Bizarre Tales

First Edition

Published by The Nazca Plains Corporation
Las Vegas, Nevada
2012

ISBN: 978-1-61098-197-2
E-book: 978-1-61098-198-9

Published by

The Nazca Plains Corporation ®
4640 Paradise Rd, Suite 141
Las Vegas NV 89109-8000

PUBLISHER'S NOTE
Bizarre Tales is a work of fiction created wholly by Christopher Trevor's imagination. All characters are fictional and any resemblance to any persons living or deceased is purely by accident. No portion of this book reflects any real person or events.

Male Cover Photo, Ekh Photo
Art Director, Blake Stephens

Bizarre Tales

First Edition

Christopher Trevor

DEDICATION

Eric and his "bizarre" erotic sandals...

CONTENTS

CONTENTS CONTINUED...

INTRODUCTION

Greetings loyal readers and greetings to all new readers of my work as well...

Within the pages of this, my latest book of erotic stories you will find some very bizarre tales, if I may say so myself. The book starts out with one of the hottest things I am drawn to, a man in uniform, or in this case, a man out of uniform, namely a studly overly macho marine named Dale, who after a night out with a few of his civilian buddies is out for breakfast in a family oriented diner and finds himself to be the main course for four trucker fuckers, as Dale comes to call them when he unwittingly meets them in the story "An Officer But Not A Gentleman."

John Robinson, another of my recurring characters, this one a handsome suited captive executive, graces us once more with his presence and another bizarre encounter in his hotel suite in "Another Excerpt from John's Chronicles."

The biggest escape for me in this book of erotic tales comes in the form of "Danny's Examination" wherein a young muscle boy jock headed for college and big dreams of football stardom winds up experiencing one of the most bizarre medical exams in history.

As you all know I am always on the lookout for new and interesting writing talent and twice more I was not disappointed. The first new author I am proud to feature in this book is my buddy Mike, the guy lifter, author of the story, "My First Lift and Carry." The second author I am proud to present to all of you is Alan Skram, author of the story "The Deputy."

Lastly, I have again honored "men in uniform" in my latest tale of discipline, "Captain Healey Takes His CP." If the name of the Captain is familiar I will only say it should be.

As always I thank all of you for your constant support, interest in my work and most of all for nurturing my strange behavior.

Happy Reading,

Christopher Trevor

AN OFFICER, BUT NOT A GENTLEMAN

Written by Christopher Trevor

This story was inspired and begun from a blog that I found on the internet while searching for pictures of men in tuxedo socks, dress socks and just plain any old kind of black socks. As luck would have it I happened across this blog entry about a marine parading around in his knee high black dress socks in public...

Have you ever sat down for breakfast with a large, tattooed marine wearing only his boxers, a stained wife beater, a sideways trucker hat, his marine uniform issued patent leather lace-up dress shoes, and his black nylon thin ribbed dress socks pulled up to just under his knees? Well, I have, and I did at a crowded family and trucker diner. And it was the marine's chosen attire that morning that was his undoing, seeing as a few of the truckers breakfasting there at the diner that morning saw the rugged and studly marine's military tattoos, his trucker hat and his prissy nylon socks and decided to have some fun with the United States serviceman. Like most people they figured that being that the oddly dressed stud was a marine he would be able to take all that they could dish out…and then some. And who of us doesn't enjoy finding out just how much a marine can take? They are made for being pushed over the edge after all…

My friend, Dale, is a marine to the fullest extent – he's actually a full blown officer in the marines. The most commonly used words in his vocabulary are "Oorah", "Semper Fi", "Beer", and any variation of the F word that just happens to pop into his (jar) head. He's built like a Pit Bull – a brick shit house to put it plainly, short, but stout, and his muscles bulge from his shirt. But all that muscle was no help to him that morning at the diner when we were having breakfast. Saying that Dale has a strong personality is like saying that a nuclear bomb is "just a little bang." He speaks in a booming, Bostonian, profane stream of consciousness. Dale was born without a filter-whatever is in his head comes barreling out of his mouth like a Mac Truck. No wonder he decided to become a marine…

He's one of the best friends and one of the funniest and most loyal people I've ever met. He's a great wingman for almost anything – to talk to girls with, to roll a party with, to play sports with, and as found out that morning at the diner, great to have repeated sexual romps with in the most heinous of situations. But there are certain things you just don't do with him. Like take him to a family diner in his skivvies, for instance.

Perry, Craig, Dale and I stopped at the diner for a heavy, greasy breakfast after our night out at a swanky dance – it had actually been a swanky ball in a seaside mansion that, for our enjoyment, had been filled to the brink with liquor. Dale was on leave from the marines, visiting his family and such, and I and Perry and Craig wanted to show our buddy a good time, but, little did we know that Dale would be getting more of a good time than he bargained for. It was the morning after, and we were all a little hung-over, Dale especially so. Dale's diner bonanza went like this:

We got out of Dale's dad's truck. The marine was wearing his boxers, a stained wife beater, a sideways trucker hat, and to top it off, his United States marine issued patent leather lace-up dress shoes and black thin ribbed nylon dress socks pulled up to just under his knees. We asked him if he was actually going to enter the diner dressed like that and he says, "Eh, fuck it buds, all I have with me is my tuxedo from last night and I don't want to mess it the fuck up, my uniform is back at my parent's house, so whatever, we're going to be sitting in a booth anyways, no one will notice.

Apparently Dale forgot about having to walk to the booth, because everyone in the diner, including a group of four burly truckers cranked their necks to stare as the pretty waitress led us to our booth in the most populated part of the diner. We were three relatively together looking young men, our average ages being nineteen and twenty (besides the wild eyes and party hair from the night before) trailing a tattooed United States Marine Corp Officer – Dale being one hundred and ninety pounds of rock solid muscle that torqued with each step he took, covered only by, literally, what was under his tuxedo the night before. As we passed booths people shook their heads in a "this generation's so screwed up" kind of way, parents shielded their kids eyes and four truckers were suddenly drooling at the sight of the marine in his skivvies, his marine issued shiny patent leather lace-up shoes and tall black dress socks.

After we were seated we all ordered coffee. Dale's stream of consciousness instantly ignited-

"SHIT MAN LAST NIGHT WAS GODDAMNED AWESOME THERE WERE SO MANY BABES, OORAH; EVEN CHICKS I USUALLY THINK ARE UGLY WERE HOT. I WAS TRYING TO HOOK IT UP WITH THAT ONE CHICK, WHAT'S HER NAME? FUCK, ANYWAYS...I DIDN'T GET TO GET MY BIG ROCKS OFF SO I'M FILLED TO THE RIM WITH BRIM, OORAH!" Dale was saying loudly and every customer in the diner could hear him, especially the four truckers that we were seated near.

No doubt they loved Dale's comment about him not having scored the night before with some female and now he was filled to the rim with his Brim. Nearly everyone was staring at us – it was a stare of loathing, fear, disgust and in four cases, absolute lust. These people literally wanted to kill us I thought. Perry, Craig, and I looked back and forth at each other awkwardly, each too loyal of friends to tell Dale to tone it down.

About five minutes later the waitress came back to take our orders. Dale piped up, "UH YA, COULD I GET SOME AHHH, SHIT LEMME THINK PRETTY LADY, TOAST, TOAST, I JUST WANT TOAST. OORAH."

After having taken all our orders the waitress left.

"YO BOYS, I'M GOING TO THE BATHROOM. GOING TO THROW UP ALL THAT FUCKING JACK I DRANK LAST NIGHT. I CAN FEEL IT SLOSHING AROUND IN MY

GODDAMNED INNARDS, OORAH!" Dale exclaimed and got to his feet.

Every customer in the diner – good, God fearing people that had been eating there for the last twenty years – focused on Dale as he strutted to the bathroom – He puffed out his massive chest, flexed his tattooed arms, tipped his trucker hat like an arrogant general that he wasn't and was completely oblivious to the fact that people found what he was wearing to be odd, or that they had heard every word he had roared since we sat down. None of us noticed however how the four truckers at the table near us quickly stood up and paid their bill right after Dale had made his way to the bathroom. After having paid their bill at the cashier in the front section of the diner one of the truckers politely asked the pretty cashier where the men's room was. They knew exactly where it was, they just wanted to appear polite and have an excuse for the four of them to head back into the diner. The three of us were still at our table divvying up sections of the newspaper and burying our heads in them, avoiding people's glances at all costs…and none of us the wiser about what was about to befall poor Dale in the men's room.

When Dale walked into the men's room the only other patron in there was a suit and tie guy just washing his hands after having urinated in one of the urinals. Dale sauntered past the guy, said "OORAH SIR" and then unceremoniously stepped into the first stall, did not close the stall door and kneeled down in front of the toilet.

"OH GAWD, I GOTTA FUCKING UPCHUCK SIR OUT THERE IN YOUR SUIT AND TIE! OORAH!" Dale called out and as he began heaving into the bowl the suit and tie guy quickly made his way out of the bathroom.

Before the bathroom door could close however the four truckers stepped in and the last one in taped an "Out of Order" sign on the door and then latched it locked behind him. They all spied Dale in the stall on his knees. Dale heaved big and loud, the contents of his stomach and all the liquor he had consumed the night before at the dance spewing out of his mouth and nose and into the toilet. With one hand pressed against the floor for balance Dale reached up and used his other hand to repeatedly flush the toilet. It was the sounds of the toilet flushing that masked the sounds of the four truckers as they chuckled meanly and sadistically, watching from outside the stall as the brawny marine emptied his stomach.

Dale farted a few times as he retched and spewed his mess into the bowl. It felt to the marine as if it would go on and on and on. On his knees with the toe sections of his shoes curled back Dale lowered his face closer to the bowl and heaved yet some more, farting and ripping real loud at that point.

"FUCKING GEEZ AND OORAH, I REALLY TIED ONE ON LAST NIGHT!" Dale said with a grin and pulled down the flusher.

When he was finally done Dale chuckled like the bonafide marine that he is, heaved a few last times and gave the flusher handle a few good tugs for good measure. As he was lifting his head away from the toilet his stomach churned and he quickly lowered his noggin again.

"OH FUCKING FUCKS," the marine swore and still more vomit erupted from him, and this time as he heaved and hawed into the bowl his trucker hat fell off and landed in the bowl, along with what was spewing from his mouth. "OH DAMN AND NO OORAH THIS TIME, MY GODDAMNED LUCKY HAT!!!"

A few moments later, finished at last emptying his stomach Dale sat up on his knees in front of the toilet, as if he was saying a prayer to the marine gods or something.

"OH MAN, THAT WAS SOME AWESOME PUKING," Dale grunted his voice sort of scratchy now as he cleared his throat and his head spun. "BUT FUCK, LOOK AT THAT SHIT, MY LUCKY GODDAMNED HAT SUBMERGED IN MY GUNK…OF ALL THINGS, HAR, HAR, FUCKING HAR, TOO BAD I DON'T GOT ME A PANSY NAVY SEAL HERE TO DIVE IN THERE AFTER IT…AND…"

But then, Dale's vulgar rant was suddenly cut off in mid-sentence when the biggest of the four truckers, a burly over-sized nearly bald guy with muscles the size of bowling balls, his nickname being Sludge reached down and into the stall. He grabbed Dale by his high and tight haircut with just the fronts of his fingers and thumb and literally hoisted the marine to his patent leather shoed feet, jiggling his head at the same time.

"H-H-HEY!!! WHAT THE FUCKS???" Dale snorted, vomit pasted to the sides of his lips as he suddenly found himself being lifted to his feet by the thin ends of his short marine style haircut. "OWWW OORAH FUCKS THAT SMARTS!!!"

"All done puking your Jack up, Soldier boy?" Sludge the trucker said directly into Dale's ear as the marine tottered on his feet, his arms flailing uselessly in front of him, his head pulled slightly back.

"I AIN'T NO GODDAMNED SOLDIER BOY, I'M A HARDCORE MARINE BUD," Dale retorted. "NOW LET THE FUCK GO OF MY HIGH AND TIGHT HAIR AND…"

But instead, Sludge simply snickered and slammed Dale against the sidewall of the stall.

"HUUUFFFFF…" Dale gasped, the wind suddenly knocked out of him.

Dale's rock hard and muscular chest took most of the blow, but then Sludge pulled the marine's head back further.

"Get ready to come in for a landing Jar head," Sludge laughed, holding Dale's hair tighter.

"AW man, what you're about to do to that serviceman ain't real nice Sludge," the second trucker, a big ornery looking black guy named Earl snickered, his thick lips showing off his fang-like white teeth. "As a matter of all facts, that is a real shitty ass thing you're about to do to him there…"

With that and with all four of the truckers laughing now Sludge slammed Dale's forehead hard against the stall wall…

"OHHH…" Dale keened; saw stars and bright lights and his head spun even more now. "FUCKER!!!"

"Still able to rant huh, Soldier boy?" Sludge asked and slammed Dale's forehead again against the stall wall, harder than the first time.

"OOOOOOFFFFFFF!!!" Dale groaned, Sludge let go of the marine's hair and he and the other three men stepped aside from the stall.

Totally exhausted from his shenanigans from the night before at the party, hung over from all he had drank, totally puked out and now with his head spinning in a reverse type of orbit and a bruise or two forming on his forehead Dale pressed his palms against the stall wall. He took a few deep breaths and then faced forward, a look of total bewilderment on his mug, and then began trying to shamble out of the stall.

"G-got to get my goddamned lucky hat out of the shitter and get back to my buds at the table," Dale whispered to no one in particular, a bit befuddled at his whereabouts at the moment.

But then, as he tried to move past Sludge it was the third trucker who took a turn at Dale next. Bruno, or as his trucker buddies called him, Big Bruno, grabbed a handful of Dale's wife beater, yanked the marine forward with it as a sort of leash and then slammed Dale back into the stall. This time Dale landed against the back wall of the stall, his body and muscular legs straddling the toilet bowl that was still filled with his last offering of puke and his lucky trucker hat. Big Bruno, built like a dump truck, also a phrase coined by his trucker buddies grinned through a set of broken and knocked out teeth, reached into the stall for the marine and again took him by a handful of his wife beater.

"FUCKIN' LET GO OF ME YOU LOUSE!!! BEATIN' ON ME LIKE THIS SURE AS ALL FUCKS AIN'T COOL YOU MEATHEADS! I'M A GODDAMNED MARINE AND YOU MUGS NEED TO RESPECT THAT AND…" Dale began but his words were again cut off as Big Bruno literally hauled him over the toilet bowl and out of the stall, Dale's shoed feet dancing stupidly and trying to gain some traction on the slippery bathroom floor at the same time.

When Bruno let go of Dale the marine went spinning against the bathroom wall, his broad shoulders taking most of the blow this time, stunning him some more…and Bruno taking Dale's wife beater, seeing as when he let go of Dale the shirt sheered right off his muscular torso. Dale stood heaving and gasping against the wall wearing nothing more now than just his white boxer shorts, black nylon knee socks and his marine issued dress shoes.

"Well, well, ain't he just the purdiest thang?" the fourth trucker, an imposing looking Spanish guy who people only knew and referred to as "The Bulge," said.

The Bulge got his nickname for that simple reason, because in his jeans, even the loose fitting ones he was always sporting a monster-sized bulge.

"I don't know about you three guys but I just LOVES me a marine in his skivvies," the Bulge said, stepping fearlessly next to Dale as he pressed himself up against the wall, trying desperately to get his bearings. "They just make the best pussies on earth…"

At The Bulge's comment all four of the truckers laughed raucously…

Stepping in front of Dale The Bulge took the marine's big fat nipples in his thumbs and first few fingers, gripped them tight and spun them hard, sending chills through Dale's massively muscular body.

"OOOOORRRRR, FUCKER, FUCKERS, FUCKERS TRUCKERS!!!" Dale suddenly piped up all loud and powerful sounding. "YOU BOYS AIN'T JUST HORSIN' AROUND HERE ARE YOU? YOU MUGS ARE FAGGOTS FOR MARINES LIKE ME!!! WELL YOU ALL CAN JUST FORGET THIS SHIT AND…"

As Dale was making ready with his ham-sized hands clenched into huge fists, ready to use his military training on the truckers, The Bulge yanked hard on the marine's pecs now and hauled him forward, searing pain in his pecs and nipples blinding the marine's thoughts and concentration.

"AAAARRRRRRHHH!!! BASTARD!!!" Dale reeled as he was slammed against the bathroom wall yet again, and this time as he landed Sludge clocked him hard on the side of the jaw and at the same time Earl, the brutish black trucker, in a blindingly fast motion grabbed the waistband of Dale's boxers and they were then around the marine's shoed and socked ankles. "HHUUUUUUUUHHH…"

Dale stood there with a hand pressed against his jaw, trying to make sense of what had just happened, and how in all fucks he had just wound up minus his wife beater and boxers, of all things…

"Now ain't he just all sexy and appealing here," Earl chortled and brazenly gave Dale's dangling soft cock a grip and twirl, beads of piss emanating from the marine's dick hole.

"UUUUUUUUHHH…N-NO PLAYIN' WITH MY FAMILY JEWELS FUCKER!!!" Dale snorted loudly, again clenching his big hands into fists, beyond determined to turn this situation around and to his advantage.

It was all just too humiliating for the well-trained marine, being beat on and humiliated out of his wife beater and boxers by four lowlife truckers…of all things…

But as Dale was preparing to throw a punch at Earl Sludge clocked him yet again on the jaw, this time sending the marine sliding down the wall…

"OOOOOOHHH…CRAPOLA!!!" Dale groaned loudly, feeling his teeth seem to vibrate in his head.

As he slid down the wall, his face showing pain Sludge and Big Bruno grabbed the marine by his huge curled biceps and back up to his shoed feet. Then, they yanked him forward and out of his boxer shorts that were at his ankles. They dragged a whimpering and cursing Dale away from the wall and to the row of sinks near the stalls. Dale was dragged on the toes sections of his shoes, his head hanging down, snot dripping out of his nose, dribbling saliva out of his mouth along with remnants of his vomit from earlier and his jaw, forehead and back of his head aching from the blows they'd been dealt. From behind his muscular butt cheeks were a sight to see as he was unceremoniously dragged along…

"WH-WHAT – what the fucks you mugs want with me eh?" Dale seethed and then when he was in front of one of the sinks Sludge and Big Bruno gripped the marine's upper arms tighter yet as Earl and The Bulge grabbed one of his socked ankles each.

Together the four men hoisted the naked but for his socks and shoes marine up onto the sink, setting him down on the edge of it, and then the marine received the answer to his question when Earl and The Bulge splayed his muscular tree-trunk like legs wide apart. Dale's pink sweaty and stinky bunghole was put on nasty display.

"OH MAN, lookit that will you?" Earl asked sounding all horned up and lusty. "My wife don't have a pussy hole that sexy…"

"FUCKING MUGS!!! PLANNING ON USING THIS MARINE AS YOUR GODDAMNED CUNT HOLE?" Dale roared now, realizing what he was in for. "Bastards, this is no way to treat a United States serviceman!!"

Dale struggled to no avail in the men's grip as Sludge let go of one of his arms, again grabbed his high and tight hair in a fist and slammed Dale's head against the mirrored wall behind him…

"HOOOOOOFFFFFF…" Dan panted and this time he nearly lost consciousness…

More than likely even a jarhead's head could only take so much…

As Dale sat there helpless and spread out on the sink Sludge stepped between the marine's spread legs as Earl and The Bulge lifted his legs a bit higher, really putting his marine stink-hole on display…

"N, no, no…" Dale whined miserably as the two men held tighter and tighter to his socked ankles.

"Coming into a diner all sexy like you were Marine and not expect four horny and underprivileged truckers not to take notice?" Sludge asked, undoing the button on his mangy jeans and shucking them down along with his briefs to his booted ankles.

In a stupor Dale saw the monster-sized cock that was aimed at his butt-hole and he cringed atop the sink.

"BASTARD, no, no man..." Dale sniveled miserably, but then felt his hole being spit in over and over.

Glancing down Sludge saw that Big Bruno was on his knees in front of the splayed marine and spitting globs of reeking diner tasting saliva into his shit chute.

"OH YEAH, that's it Big Bruno, moisten and sweeten up this marine's hole for me," Sludge said with a grin. "...cause he's gonna really need to be slicked up back there when I start plowing into him..."

As he spoke Sludge held his big cock in hand, cupping his cum filled balls with the other. Dale was mortified as his hole was used as a spittoon by the man called Big Bruno...and he also realized that The Bulge and Earl were kneading and caressing his black socked calves...

Dale's cock began to betray him by stiffening between his legs...

"Fuckers, lowlife trucker fuckers, lemme the hell out of this two bit men's room huh???" Dale pleaded and gripped the sides of the sink as he suddenly felt Bug Bruno's tongue lapping and licking at his exposed shit chute. "OOOOOOOOOOOOO..."

"Fucking fucks, he likes that Bruno..." Sludge laughed as his hard cock dripped droplets of pre cum. "OH yeah, you like having your anal canal eaten huh Jar head?"

"N-NO, NO..." Dale ranted and arched himself further forward on the sink, almost presenting his asshole to Sludge now...

On his knees Big Bruno gripped Dale's muscled ass cheeks and buried his face in his asshole...

"AAARRRRRHHH..." Dale cried out in man's passion and his cock then grew harder, to epic proportions almost. "OORAH!!!"

Sludge simply leered at the captured marine and said, "Knew it when you walked in the diner Jar head..."

"So glad you knew what you knew asshole," Dale reeled as he gripped the sides of the sink tighter, his legs being lifted higher yet by his socked ankles.

When he looked to his sides he saw that The Bulge and Earl were now kissing and licking his patent leather marine issued dress shoes, squeezing his black socked ankles at the same time, stealing sniffs at his socks also... Finally, when his asshole was as wet as duck's bottom Big Bruno got to his feet and Sludge aimed his thick veined hard cock at the marine's dripping asshole. He entered the marine with a sound like SPLAT as he speared inside him...

"OOOOOHHH HOLY CRAPOLA!!!" Dale thundered atop the sink. "Got a fucker trucker using me like some cheap whore on a Saturday night! AAARRRHHH..."

Dale arched his head back and Sludge began a slow and then fast and then slow and then fast thrusting rhythm as he slid his huge tube-steak in and out of the marine's asshole.

"OH FUCK yeah, you are this morning's pussy Jar head," Sludge grunted and his trucker buddies laughed meanly.

Dale clenched his teeth and then the pulpy tube of meat between his own thighs betrayed him by stiffening to a hard-on all his own, marine sized as he and his buddies at his base would have said. In growing horror and disbelief Dale felt his massive sized man meat hardening and then it was standing at attention.

"EEEERRRRRRRR...FUCKING BASTARD, taking such liberties!!!" Dale seethed and then the truckers all noticed his steely erection as it bounced and flounced between his tree-trunk like muscular thighs and flopped against his six pack abs.

Dale's lower back slid over the sink he was perched on and then humiliatingly, he felt it...a geyser of cum was about to erupt from his pulsing and throbbing male member.

"OOOOHHH, NO, GAWD..." the hardcore marine sputtered and arched his head back further. "FUUUUCCCKKKSSS..."

Private First class marine Dale Taylor felt his cheeks flush with shame as the man called Sludge savagely fucked his ass, reaming him it felt like, and the other guys at his sides, GODDAMN IT ALL, licking his marine shoes and kissing his damned socked ankles and calves...but the real shame the marine felt was when his stored up load of spunk erupted from his dick hole and spurted and splashed all over his stomach region, his massive muscular chest, his nipples and even up to and onto his neck...

"OOOOOOOO FUCKERS," Dale prattled and as his head spun and as he shot his load he gripped the sides of the sink tighter, balancing himself as now the pain from being fucked was astronomical. "OOOOHHRRR my poor shit chute..."

"Damn, did you see that?" Earl asked as he held one of Dale's socked ankles to his lips. "Fucking pussy boy marine shot his load while being fucked like some horny teenage girl.

"Yeah, FUCK YEAH," Sludge groaned and with an animal cry jammed his lean, sinewy hips forward, his butt muscles clenched tight and squeezed together, and drove his throbbing tube steak all the way in to the marine's seeming wanting ass hole. "The marine must be one of those fuckers who shoots his load whenever his hole is porked, I heard of sluts like him... HA!!! And by the time we're done with him he'll have emptied his goddamned gonads a few times over...OORAH for you Jar head...OOOOHHH!!!"

"Yeah, and seeing as he cums when his hole is porked we don't even need to jack him off," Big Bruno laughed, holding Dale's other foot and calf like it was an ear of corn and nibbling on it.

As Dale's cum dripped down his chest and his stomach and into his pubic bush he grunted miserably when he felt Sludge's deeply-buried rod spurting out his own slugs of scalding jazz, right up and into his rectum. Dale felt it in his chute like a warm flood... and to his embarrassment his cock erupted a final spurt of cum as well.

"OOOOOHHH..." was the sound of Dale and Sludge as they sated themselves.

As soon as he caught his breath Sludge withdrew his softening, cum and saliva coated cock from the marine's asshole. Earl and The Bulge let go of Dale's ankles and calves and let them drop to the sides of the sink. Dale sat, literally in the sink now as Sludge panted breathlessly and he himself did the same...

"Fucking lowlifes, you guys had your fun with me..." Dale began and pressed his hands against the sides of the top of the sink. "Time for me to retrieve my lucky goddamned hat from the shitter over there, get me my wife beater and boxers back and be on my way and..."

But then, Sludge and Earl each very quickly grabbed one of the marine's huge arms each and gave them a mean twist.

"OWWW, what in all hell???" Dale panted miserably as he was hoisted up again so that his asshole was back on display.

The marine's eyes opened as wide as two saucers and in horror when he looked down and saw the trucker called Big Bruno hoisting his legs up by his ankles this time, so that his knees were nearly in his face.

"OH HOLY SHIT AND REAL CRAPOLA!!" the marine railed and then the sore walls of his asshole seemed to suck Big Bruno's cock inside him. "UUUUHHH…"

The marine's ass lips were raw from the pounding that Sludge had given them and the thick slabs of his pectorals rose and fell now with his heavy breathing as he was thoroughly butt fucked yet again. This time the bottoms of the marine's marine issued shoes were looking at the ceiling as the wearer of them endured a second reaming. Dale was in a most uncomfortable and mortifying position for a marine of his caliber. Sludge and Earl held his huge arms tight, keeping them twisted at the sides, forcing the marine not to move as he was butt-fucked a second time… The Spanish thug known as The Bulge was stroking his hard crank, awaiting his turn next at that morning's pussy hole…

"AAAARRRRHHH Fucking truckers are all pigs…no respect…" Dale seethed as his still hard cock rubbed against his stomach and his balls pressed between his splayed thighs.

As he was fucked deep and hard by Big Bruno the marine felt his balls churning in his sweaty and mangy sac.

"OH NO NAW, not again, OH YOU FUCKERS," Dale ranted and felt it, as he was about to geyser again from his dick hole. "Trucker fuckers…"

"What's the matter you pussy holed marine, you don't like pecker meat up your wazoo?" Big Bruno asked Dale mockingly, gripped his socked calves tighter and plowed deeper inside him.

"You bastards," Dale reeled miserably as his cock churned now. "I'll make you guys pay for this…you'll see…OHHH FUUUUCCCKKK…"

"Pay for it pussy marine?" Big Bruno asked breathlessly as he felt his own load about to erupt. "Thanks to you walkin' into the diner in your prissy socks and underwear we're getting it all for free…HARRRR!!!"

But then, as Big Bruno shot his thick load of soup into Dale's asshole the marine let out a guttural cry and also spewed his second load…

"OH FUCK, it hurts buds, IT FUCKING HURTS, where are my buds to rescue me when I need 'em huh???" Dale cried out and all four of the truckers laughed meanly, Big Bruno laughing breathlessly as he deposited his sperm inside the marine… "If my marine buds and brothers were here they would kill you trucker fuckers for this shit…"

As Big Bruno's shriveling cock exited the marine's asshole Dale's butt showed the remnants of sloppy drippings of cum as it landed in the sink. As he was held tight and fast The Bulge wasted no time…

While Dale was spewing the last of his second mess of sperm all over his stomach area where his marine sized cock was pressed against the Spanish guy known as "The Bulge" stepped up to the marine next. He took Dale's socked calves from Big Bruno and spread them wider apart.

"AWWW no, no, not you too you fucking street looking thug," Dale spat at "The Bulge."

But it was when "The Bulge's" cock speared its way inside Dale that the pain became something that the young well-muscled and overly macho marine never knew before.

"AWWW FUCK AND ALL THE GODS IN THEIR HEAVENS!" Dale roared as "The Bulge" thrust into him most savagely.

The back of Dale's closely shaved head slammed against the bathroom mirror and his held up legs were gyrating with a life all their own, not to mention that the hardcore marine's legs were as numb as stumps at that point from having been held in such an awkward position for such a length of time.

"You bastards, I'll kill you fucker truckers for this myself…" Dale sobbed then. "Let go of me, get that missile out of my shit chute and you'll see…you all will see…"

But the four truckers only laughed at Dale's impotent threats and "The Bulge" slammed long and hard and fat into the marine's rectum, over and over and over again, tearing him apart back there it felt to Dale…

"Yeah, yeah, we'll see about all that you sexy marine," "The Bulge" said in his Spanish accent and slid in and out of Dale's hole like it was a pussy. "But meanwhile after I cum my good buddy Earl is next at this sweet hole of yours. OORAH marine…"

"YIIIHHH!!!" was Dale's retort as his cock, still hard and the marine in disbelief over that spurted a very small mess of his cum again…as he was thoroughly and well fucked.

Dale glanced up and saw that the bottoms of his shoes seemed to be smiling up at the ceiling…his heart broke and his ass ached and his cock dribbled…

And then, before the literally fucked marine knew what was happening, "The Bulge" was spewing his hot cum into Dale's hole…

While Dale was having his asshole plowed more than a farm field me, Perry and Craig were wondering what was taking our marine buddy so long in the men's room. I mean, really, how long does it take for a marine to throw up all the liquor he drank just hours before? While we were sipping coffee and reading the sections of newspaper that we had divvied up between us the waitress came over to tell us that our food was just about ready and did we want to be served then or wait for our friend to return from the men's room. I looked at Perry and Craig and shrugged. We all agreed to wait for Dale to return from the men's room, if it wasn't too much of a problem for the waitress. She said it was no problem whatsoever and left the table. So, while none of us were the wiser to the embarrassments and miseries that Dale was suffering in the men's room we simply resumed sipping coffee and reading the newspaper.

After "The Bulge" had spewed his hot Spanish cum into our marine buddy's hole he lowered Dale's legs slowly, and then squatted down in front of him. Seconds later Dale was moaning and groaning and gripping the sides of the sink he was splayed on as the Spanish thug slithered his monster-sized tongue into the marine's cum soaked rear end.

"HOOOOOOO OORAH, that fucking guy is eating my hole like it was a damned buffet," Dale grunted from deep in his throat as "The Bulge" ate the remnants of cum that he and his buddies had thus far deposited into the sex captive marine.

But then, before Dale could make heads of tails or what was happening it was Big Bruno and Sludge holding his arms twisted and at the sides of the sink as the big black trucker named Earl next grabbed the marine's socked calves and began hoisting them upwards. Once more Dale's hole was being put on awful display and the bottoms of his marine issued shoes were once again looking up at the ceiling.

"NO, NO, not again, OH MAN, my poor hole, OORAH!" Dale ranted and clenched his ass cheeks tightly together.

There was no way he was going to cop another joint in his hole. But the black trucker seemed to be expert at opening up topnotch and tough guy marines; Earl was not going to accept "no" for an answer. The black trucker delivered some resounding and loud slaps to the marine's ass cheeks and then when Dale was nearly crying in pain from having just been spanked like a misbehaved kid he felt two of Earl's big black fingers wedging and digging his hole apart.

"Ah, and there we go you pretty marine, such a nice hole you had under wraps just for me huh?" Earl asked the marine mockingly.

Once more tears welled up in the big butch marine's eyes as he was forced to accept yet another hard cock into his most private crevice. As Dale cried tears of anger, rage and shame his cock went semi hard and dribbled out beads of piss this time, seeing as he was unable to shoot another marine-sized load at that point.

"Oh yeah, that's more like it you pretty marine," the black trucker chuckled as he held tight to Dale's socked calves and plowed in and out of the guy with a speed that bordered on bionic.

Earl breathed heavily as he pounded the back of Dale's head against the mirror he was propped up against with each virile thrust of his powerfully muscled butt.

"Oh man, you are really turning into a class-A bathroom whore man," Earl said and he and his three buddies laughed meanly.

After Dale pissed out what was left of his marine cum he recovered himself somewhat and was consumed with utter humiliation and shame at having been so thoroughly bested by four lowlife truckers. He was a hardcore marine and should have been able to take these guys with one hand tied behind him, but here he was, completely at their mercy. His manly pride was beginning to feel shattered...but NO, inwardly he would not allow that. His marine buds had hazed him in worse ways than this when he had first joined up, so this was just another test of his manhood...or so the marine thought and felt his shriveled cock churning yet again as Earl announced that he was cumming at that point.

"OOOOHHH fuck yeah, FUCKING A, fucking pretty marine," Earl seethed, gripped Dale's socked calves tighter, really digging his fingers in and jammed his spewing cock deep into the marine's bowels.

The other three guys clapped and hooted as Dale cried miserably in a marine's pain as Earl emptied his balls into the serviceman's hole. He pounded like a jackhammer every time another rope of his slop erupted from him...

Finally, when he was done, Earl's big black cock slowly slid out of Dale's hole...

The other three truckers let go of Dale and the marine simply sat there on the sink, his legs dangling now as he breathed heavily, cum dripping out of his ass and into the sink. He watched miserably and with humiliation as the four truckers pulled up their jeans, zipped and belted up and prepared to exit the diner's restroom.

"HOOOOO, that was some fucking," the trucker named Sludge said as he and the other three headed toward the door to the men's room.

"You said it man, my cock feels real good right about now," the Spanish guy called "The Bulge" said and squeezed his spent cock through his jeans.

The four truckers turned to look at Dale as he slowly began prying himself off the sink, as massive sized droplets of trucker splooge and "The Bulge's" saliva dripped some more from his rectal hole.

"Boy oh boy and man oh man, we sure as all fuck filled that marine didn't we?" Big Bruno asked as he and his buddies watched their mess drip from Dale's hole and into the sink.

"Fuckers truckers..." Dale whimpered and to the shock of the four trucker rapists the marine grabbed his joystick and began stroking himself, he was hard as steel in no time.

"Holy fuck, jeez, lookit that shit, don't believe what I'm seein' there," the four truckers murmured to themselves as Dale stroked his big cock.

After the waitress could not hold our order anymore she delivered our food, just as Dale finally got back to the table, missing his hat and walking slightly bowlegged... His wife beater was in tatters but still wearable, he was in his boxers but as he approached the table I realized that on his feet he was wearing just his marine issued shoes, his tall black up to the knee dress socks were gone.

"OH HELL YEAH, MY TOAST," Dale said as he sat down. "OORAH, YOU KNOW BOYS YOU WOULD NEVER BELIEVE WHAT THE FUCKING FUCK JUST HAPPENED WHILE I WAS IN THE LATRINE..."

From that moment on he was dead silent, hungry all of a sudden it seemed and focused on his toast like a sniper. He wolfed it down like there was no tomorrow. I noticed that as he sat eating in silence that he was squirming a bit on his seat. But all good things, as they say, must end and Dale started back up. It was as if he had been pondering and mulling over just how much he should tell us of his ordeal in the diner bathroom.

"DUDES, SO WHEN I JUST THREW UP IN THERE, DAMN, MY FUCKING TRUCKER HAT FELL INTO THE

GODDAMNED TOILET," Dale barked and at that moment the bathroom door in the back swung open and the four truckers who had raped our marine buddy exited the men's room. "THERE WAS ALL THIS THROW-UP ALL OVER MY DAMNED HAT. BUT THAT HAT WAS COOL MAN, SO FUCKING COOL THAT I'M NOT THROWING IT AWAY OVER SOME PUKE. SO UH, AFTER SOME DUDES GOT OVER A BIT ON ME I FISHED THE HAT OUT. I RINSED IT OFF AND THEN LASHED IT TO THE HAND DRYER WITH ONE OF MY SOCKS TO LET IT DRY."

As the four truckers made their way past our table they all smirked at Dale. So at that moment I knew that Dale had used one of his tall socks to lash his hat to the hand dryer in the men's room, but I had to wonder what had become of the sock's mate.

"SO WHATEVER YOU BOYS DO, DON'T LET ME FORGET TO GET MY HAT BEFORE WE LEAVE HERE HUH?" Dale went on, munching a mouthful of toast as he spoke. "OORAH! SO ANYWAYS, ABOUT THAT FUCKING…"

And as the truckers left the diner I saw that the one called "The Bulge" had a long black sock sticking out of his back pocket, sort of like a bandanna. And at that same moment was when we cut Dale off in his vulgar tirade. People were staring at us in horror, none of them aware of what the marine who served their country had just endured in the men's room. In unison, I, Perry and Craig said things like, "There are families here." Dale looked around, seemed to squirm a bit more in his chair and said, "OH SHIT, SORRY," responding as he looked back and forth only to realize that every person in the diner was watching the Dale show, and not to mention that they wanted to turn it off…with a pitchfork. Dale watched as the four truckers left the diner, a look of marine intensity etched on his handsome mug. I didn't ask why one of the marine's dress socks was hanging out of the back pocket of the jeans of the guy called "The Bulge."

After he was done scoffing down his toast Dale leaned in and said, "Boy's get the check," and buried himself in a newspaper.

As we walked out of the diner about ten minutes later, we were all thinking we were about to be followed, beaten, then tar and feathered in front of the local city hall. An old curmudgeon who had been giving us particularly angry looks all during breakfast yelled out, "Hey, Marine, don't forget your hat," and threw the hat to Dale with a chuckle. Dale thanked the guy and as we left the diner and headed for the pick-up Dale pulled his lone tall black sock out of the hat, which he had used to tie the hat to the hand dryer. Once more I didn't ask my buddy what had become of his other black dress sock...

But that's the thing about marines – Dale in particular. No matter what they do, no matter what's done to them, you've got to respect and even like them at some level...

ANOTHER EXCERPT FROM "JOHN'S CHRONICLES"

Written by Christopher Trevor and his muse, John

In my last book "Men in Peril 3" I introduced readers to the character of John Robinson, a ruggedly handsome and staunch business executive who unwittingly stumbles into a perilous situation while on a recent business excursion. As stated in the introduction for the excerpt from "John's Chronicles" in my book "Men In Peril 3" this story started out much like "Timmy's Ticklish Trials" did, as an e-mail and IM exchange between two kinky and very horny men on the internet. When John Robinson told me of his fetish for being bound up and held captive while wearing nothing more than his executive style under shorts and dark colored dress socks, what he sometimes refers to as his power socks, I have to say that my interest in him was piqued. Seeing as I always thought of men in dark colored socks as submissive and somehow vulnerable all this talk about those dark colored nylon stinkers made me wonder just how staunch and rugged a guy wearing them could be. But even my artist buddy Joe T. once said that a guy's black socks are powerful somehow, although that irrational and erotic part of me disagreed totally. So, John Robinson and I began relating fantasies back and forth until we hit upon one that seems to have gone on for some time. In his fantasy John Robinson is a senior banking executive on a business trip in an unnamed city and staying in a suite in an unnamed luxury hotel. With him on this particular business trip is a group of his protégés, what John Robinson calls his underlings, or perhaps his up and coming junior executives. The junior executives of course do not get to share John Robinson's luxury suite; that will be his private domain, his sanctuary, his refuge from work stress, and it will also be the place of his captivity when he unwittingly befriends a gentleman he meets at the hotel bar upon his arrival there. The gentleman already seated at the bar when John sits down next to him decked out in a thousand dollar suit by Armani sees in John a man who thoroughly enjoys a challenge and a man who would stick to his end of a bargain no matter what the stakes. John's body language, his careful and corporate attire and his entire demeanor speak volumes to this. The two men start up a conversation about why John is at the hotel (he explains that his company sent him on an annual business seminar which usually lasts two weeks or so and the hotel maintains an account with the company so John always receives the best treatments the hotel can offer) and why the unnamed gentleman is there as well. While the gentleman never really says for sure why he is at the hotel, other than it is sort of work related, he does manage to move the conversation over to what John loves the most in life, a good challenge. The two men clink their drink glasses to "a good challenge" and John makes the mistake of telling this stranger that in his thirty something years he has handled and wrangled his way through some really sticky situations and challenges in the business world. This opens the door for the unnamed gentleman to present John with a challenge that will be totally new to him and not just of the business world. John makes the mistake of saying "Try me," and the man says that before John has to head off to his first meeting (which John has stated will start in the hotel conference room in about an hour and a half) that he will present the topnotch executive with a challenge that will knock his socks off. At the mention of his power socks John's interest is truly elevated. When the man tells John that he more than likely would not be able to handle it and is about to walk off after finishing his drink John makes the mistake of pleading with the guy to tell him what the challenge is and no matter what it is he will be able to work his way through it. The man chuckles and says that rather than working his way through it, that John would have to work his way out of it. Now the executive's interest is piqued off the Richter scale. The man again tells John that he would not be able to handle it and starts to walk away. John steps in front of the stranger and asks to at least be told what this mysterious challenge would be, stating that nothing knocks his power socks off, stating that he wears his power socks good and tight and usually pretty tall. The man chuckles again and says two words that will change John's life forever. "Bondage Games." John is at first aghast and nearly does jump out of his wingtips so that his power socks can be knocked off, but he quickly gathers himself and his wits together and decides to plunge in further, to see what this man means by a challenge of "Bondage Games." The stranger tells John that it's really very simple, he gets to tie John up and all John has to do is get loose in the time that they will allot for the game. If John does not get loose in the allotted time then the man gets to tie him up again...in a different position. John laughs raucously as he cannot believe he has been presented with such a strange and most unusual challenge, but nonetheless it is a challenge and the executive knows that he has never been one to walk away from any challenge... John says that he would try it, adding that he has a suite in the hotel where they would have plenty of room and that being that his first meeting is still an hour and a half away that it would be a good way to kill time. To seal the deal the stranger and John shake hands and the man tells John that he must stick to his word as a gentleman and adhere to the rules of the game. As John vigorously pumps the man's hand in his he says that he is not just a businessman and executive, but that he is a man of his word at all times. The man let's go of John's hand and he tells the executive that he needs to go to his room to get his "Bondage Gear" and that he will be at John's suite shortly. John gives the man his suite number and before walking off the man gives John one last set of instructions. He tells the executive to be wearing nothing more than his underpants and socks, shoes optional, for when he will be tied up, seeing as he would not want to ruin John's expensive suit. The superlative executive is left standing there stunned and feeling as if his power socks have just been knocked off after all. Grinning wickedly John heads to his suite for this most uncommon challenge. He feels somehow a foreboding yet strangely thrilled, for he knows in his heart of hearts that he will be loose very quickly once the guy ties him up the first time...or so he thinks...

"OHHH JEEZ Louise," John Robinson muttered miserably as the water seeped into his rectum as he stood with his hands tightly roped behind him in the huge bathroom of his luxury hotel suite, a length of hose attached to the sink's water faucet and the other end of it burrowed up into his asshole, his executive shit chute if you would. "Fuck it all Mister, how much fluid are you going to fill up my rectum with?"

The man, known only to the hapless executive as "His Captor" chuckled a bit sadistically and said, "A half-gallon perhaps John? Maybe more…"

John squirmed on his feet, the tile floor beneath him…

"YUHHH, I'm aching here Mister," John gulped, sweating in the navy blue OTC ribbed nylon socks he wore along with his white executive briefs with the hole cut in the back of them to allow the hose entry into his most private sanctum.

As the cold water seeped more and more into him, the faucet set on a slow trickle John took a deep breath, hoisted himself up miserably to his socked tiptoes and danced stupidly in place, grimacing behind the cloth blindfold tied over his eyes.

"I can actually hear the water chugging around inside you John," the captor laughed meanly now as he rubbed the captive executive's stomach area.

"Chugging? Man, I'm fucking gurgling here…" John responded and had the hose not been stuffed up his a-hole he would have farted real loud and smelly, seeing as the need to do so was immense feeling.

As the water seeped colder into him John clenched his muscular ass muscles around the invasive hose, making sounds like "RRRRRRRRRRRRR RRRRRRRRRRRRR" from deep in his throat as his captor tweaked his nipples with his thumbs and fingers. Even though he was blindfolded the muscular handsome executive tried to somehow draw back from the other man's erotic and brazen touch. The feeling of his sensitive sensitized nipples being played with caused his cock to twitch and dance in his white briefs. John stood even higher on his socked tiptoes now as the cold water was starting to make him feel bloated.

"UUUUUHHHRRRRR, because of that cold water you're filling me with it's made my damned tits bubble up on my chest Mister," the executive croaked. "I always had fleshy nubs but as you can see, *and as I can't see because of this damned blindfold you got on me*, they're all fat and pliable now. EEHHHRRRRRRRRR, and you're taking full advantage of those tits by toying with them... SHIT!"

Sweat broke out everywhere on the handsome banker's muscular body, and, unknown to his captor it had loosened the ropes on his wrists behind him.

"OH yes John, very fleshy nubs, womanly tits in a way," the executive's captor laughed. "Just the way I want them prepared and prepped for your underlings when they arrive here shortly."

At the sound of his underlings coming to have at him yet again John's jaw dropped behind his blindfold, but more importantly he realized that his wrist bindings had loosened up and he had a chance at escape here...at last...at long last...

"Okay John, it looks to me like the water inside you is doing just what I wanted, it's nice and cool and as you said it has made your tits really bubble up...and they're ready for surgery I would say."

"S-surgery?" John blurted and stood flat on his socked feet as he took his chance at escape and started using his fingertips to begin undoing the knots in the ropes around his wrists.

Once again, to keep his captor occupied so he could work at getting the ropes undone John blurted out, "Surgery?" and his captor chose that moment to whip the blindfold off him. Glancing down after his vision had adjusted back to the light of the bathroom John saw a line of needles laid out on the vanity.

"SHIT!!" the executive ranted and then glanced down at his very erect nipples and saw that they had bubbled up to twice or perhaps even three times their size.

"Your underlings will be performing the surgery John," the captor teased him meanly and then leaned down to steal a long loud suck and slurp at one of his captive's oversized nubs.

As John rocked on his socked feet and did his best to hold the water in his innards in check the man with seemingly no name turned off the water faucet, stopping the flow into the executive's rectum. John rocked some more on his socked feet, on his heels and panted miserably. Actually he was practically crying at that point.

"God, there's so much water in me man," John grunted.

"Need to piss some out John?" the executive's captor asked him mockingly and gripped one his arms to move him toward the toilet bowl.

But John knew that if the man moved him, particularly if he stepped behind him to move him along he would see the loosened ropes on his wrists, SHIT, what to do? But then, John heard the door to his suite open and then slam closed.

"Hey Boss man, we're here!" the executive heard one of his underlings call out, a guy named Paul who was still sort of new to the company called out merrily. "We can't wait to see how your buddy got those tits of yours worked up for us!"

"Yeah, some buddy I got here," John murmured and looked down at the needles laid out on the vanity in total trepidation.

Then, as the ropes around his wrists loosened some more John said to himself, "Gotta make my move now," but alas, as his captor moved him away from the wall he had been propped up against while being filled with water the man noticed the loosened ropes. He quickly whirled John around stupidly on his socked toes and meanly said, "Oh no you don't bud, not yet at least..." And with that he grabbed the ends of the dangling ropes and tugged them tight back about the victimized executive's wrists. John struggled fruitlessly and miserably as the man crossed his wrists back behind him and tied them, angry at himself for not getting loose sooner, his blasted luck lately. The executive's ass cheeks looked all sexy as he danced around struggling, up again on his socked tiptoes and sweating, the tip of his cock in his briefs touching the cold tile wall. John was utterly dismayed as the man tied his wrists tighter this time. He heard the man chuckling meanly and hung his head in outright shame and misery, thinking how things like this were not supposed to happen to topnotch executives such as him.

The chugging and gurgling sounds erupted more-so from the executive's water-bloated stomach, providing entertaining sounds for John's captor and for his arriving underlings as well.

"Thought you would get loose that time huh John?" the executive's captor asked his handsome prey and this time grabbed both of his arms from behind the again thwarted executive, holding him tight, almost lovingly against himself.

He moved John again toward the toilet bowl so the guy could piss...and as John pissed, and as his captor held him tight and watched him piss, John felt totally and utterly humiliated. But the feeling was magnified a thousand times a moment later when his two underlings came sauntering into the bathroom. As John urinated the sounds of his piss as it landed in the bowl was somehow intoxicating to him. Standing flat on his socked feet again as the man who had so expertly thrust him into this heinous situation held his arms tight he pissed out what felt like gallons of fluid. As the two office underlings entered the bathroom John looked at them desperately, humiliated in front of them, he was their boss after all.

"Oh fuck man, you got better tits than my girl," the guy named Paul said as he took in the sight of his boss's jutted up fleshy nipples. "And I got to tell you Boss man; she loved it when I pierced them for her."

In response John's ass made gurgling sounds...

"OH NO, OH NO!!!" John barked and his captor quickly yanked the hose from his hole, tore his white briefs off him and sat the hapless executive unceremoniously down on the toilet.

Piss came out of John Robinson's rectum at the same time he pissed through his penis, all of this right in front of the man he called "Captor" and his two underlings. The two underlings laughed meanly and hysterically watching their boss man piss uncontrollably from two sides. John heaved in anguish as he sat on the bowl and at the same time he hemmed over the fact that his man-sized nipples seemed to jut up even more. But it was when the executive heard his captor say, "I suggest you fill him up three more times before you get to work piercing his tits, that way they'll be real pliable for your razor sharp pins," that he looked up next in outright horror.

"I'll just leave you in your two worker's capable hands now John," the executive's captor said, leaned down and squeezed one of his captive's nipples to say good-bye.

"OOOOOOOO..." John moaned and splashed some more fluid out of his asshole and dick and into the bowl he was seated on.

The scent in the bathroom was overpowering yet erotic somehow at the same time...

A few moments later John found himself bent over the sink with the length of hose back up and in his hole, courtesy this time of his sadistic and rebellious underlings. The two junior executives were taking turns pissing into the other end of the hose and John felt their warm stream invading him.

"Bastards, bastards," the executive whispered and his dick was hard as steel, no longer emanating piss but betraying him nonetheless, his balls swollen.

A while later, after having filled their boss three more times with water and as much piss that they could stream into the hose in his asshole, and after watching and listening to the executive fart and piss his brains out from two ends while he sat on the bowl with his hands secured behind him, the two underlings now had the John Hamm looking executive standing up, him a bloated heaving and high socked mess, standing there sweating and in their power…at their mercy. The two underlings stood at their boss's sides, a razor sharp needle in each of their hands, deciding on how to insert them in his jutted up nipples.

John was filled to the brim and gurgling yet again, his cock was rock hard, his balls tight and swollen.

"Let's start with the tips of his tits and then work on the outsides next," Paul said to his buddy.

"OH FUCK NO…" John pleaded as the two underlings pressed the tips of their needles against his fleshy and erect nubs, teasing them, dimpling them.

John was by now more than sweating in his so-called power socks. He again hoisted himself to his toes as the needles slowly skewered his tits. The executive's head spun.

"OHHH…pain you guys…" John moaned, as the pressure of the needles in his tits was immense.

His eyes crossed in his head and he sarcastically said, "You boys sure as fuck know that you're doing your job right here." The two underlings laughed meanly and picked up a second pin each.

"FUCK, FUCK, I'm your boss; you guys can't do this to me!!" John blubbered and screeched as the two underlings pressed the second needles against the tender meat of the sides of his nipples.

With one push each the needles were in… As John screamed in pain his two underlings used cold soaked washcloths to wipe up the small spots of blood that formed on his pierced tits.

"You boys are getting a shitty thrill doing this to the boss eh?" John asked, pressing his head against the wall and looking upwards with his teeth clenched in agony.

Without realizing it and because he had been so filled up rectally, the executive pissed downward, his cock shriveled, his urine landing on his socks.

"OOOOOO humiliating!" the executive barked woefully and from the living room of his hotel suite his captor heard his pitiful cries as the third needles were inserted in the flesh of his tits. "OH GOD!!!"

As his tits were skewered and as blood trickled down his chest John stood there over the bowl crying and pissing out what felt like gallons, looking back and forth at his two office boys…

"Fuckers, torturing me in the bathroom "surgery suite" of my luxury hotel suite," John blubbered incoherently, looking down at the needles piercing the tender flesh of his nipples.

When John's two underlings were done there were five needles each piercing each of the executive banker's nipples. John's head spun, he saw stars flashing in front of his eyes and he tottered around on his socked feet. To keep him from passing out the two underlings forced their boss to sniff RUSH, one bottle each in each of his nostrils. John Robinson, super executive then felt his heart beating super-fast. The feeling of pain mixed with ecstasy was beyond INTENSE. The smell of the RUSH seemed to make the banker's head spin in a reverse orbit. Memories of when he was a younger man in the club scene and sniffing RUSH came to him as he involuntarily snorted some more of his underling's offerings. Then, as he stood there with his head arched back, swooning in pain and ecstasy John felt the areolas of his nipples being circled with something that had a pointy end on it. He looked down through hazy vision and saw that one of his underlings, Paul was using a pin to make circles around and around his pierced nipples. DAMN, and there were still more pins laid out on the vanity. As he murmured, "Bastard, making artwork on my chest," his other underling quickly shoved the two bottles of RUSH once more into the executive's nostrils. John inhaled and his head spun away some more…the feeling of his nipples being very slowly pierced vertically now making him scream out. He took heaving big breaths and was enraptured some more in the haze of RUSH. John felt as if his nipples swelled up even more with each pin that was meanly inserted. He found himself heaving his chest forward, almost as if he were suddenly presenting his nipples to his two sadist underlings…

After a while more, perhaps a good half hour at most all that could be seen of the executive's nipples were needles on his chest, rather than nipples. John's underlings stepped back and watched the heated spectacle of their boss as he roared in anguish. As the two underlings laughed they both high-fived each other on having done a superb job skewering the boss's nipples and turning them into a work of art. Then they watched as their boss stood in front of the bathroom's full length mirror dancing in pain from socked foot to socked foot, sweating in his anguish and RUSH high…

Just then, John's captor came into the luxurious bathroom and said, "John, I'll untie your hands now," and John turned and looked at his captor in disbelief, while at the same moment his two underlings walked nonchalantly out of the bathroom.

"So you yourself can take out the pins," John's captor explained, for the reason that he would untie his executive captive. "How do you feel about that bud?"

In response John simply glowered at his captor...

The man stepped into the bathroom, squatted down in front of the executive and John watched as the guy ceremoniously lifted one of his feet off the floor. John balanced himself on one foot as the guy slid his OTC navy blue sock off him, followed by doing the same thing with his other foot. After untying the executive's hands he walked out of the bathroom, carrying John's long socks with him...another trophy of sorts it seemed...or perhaps just getting ready to put him in a fresh pair of his power socks for the next round of bondage, once he got all the pins out of his tits that is...

Looking down as his head continued to spin the poor executive didn't know which pin to pull out first... He simply decided to make an executive decision...

From the living room of the suite the executive's captor heard the sounds of John Robinson crying and swearing as he pulled the pins out of his pierced tits...and he readied the restraints to tie his prize yet again...

DANNY'S EXAMINATION

Written by Christopher Trevor

"I don't know why you had to come with me Dad," Danny said to his father as they sat in the waiting room of Doctor Rack's office and well-equipped lab. "I mean, I just turned nineteen years old two days ago for Pete's sake. Getting a medical examination is something that I think I can handle on my own at this point."

"I'm sure you can," Mr. Smith said to his handsome and muscular football player son. "It's just that this exam is for your college football scholarship and I want to make sure the doc here goes over you real well."

Danny grimaced with a look of self-consciousness etched on his square jawed, finely chiseled good-looking face.

"Huh, I really don't relish the thought of my *dad* watching as the doctor examines me," Danny said. "I mean since I was like twelve years old I've been going to the doctor on my own. Now all of a sudden when I'm at the age of nineteen my dad wants to supervise me being examined, jeez."

"Hey, it could be worse," Mr. Smith said to his son.

"Really, how?" Danny asked, turning his face to his father, a sly looking grin on his face.

"Your mother could have come with you," the older man responded and he and his son both laughed heartily, the older man ruffling his son's short cropped dirty blond hair.

Like most football player's Danny sported a very short, almost marine-like haircut, what most marines call high and tight. Just then they saw a man dressed in a suit emerge from Doctor Rack's lab. He stepped over to the pretty receptionist at the front desk to take care of his CO pay and to set up a follow up appointment.

"I got to tell you, that Doctor Rack is the best," the business suited man said to the receptionist. "Every time I come here for an exam I feel like I've really been given great treatment."

"Yes, Doctor Rack is very special," the receptionist said agreeably.

"Man, she's really pretty," Danny murmured, glancing at the red headed twenty something year old receptionist (and the handsome man in the suit as well) as she processed the executive's information.

"You always seemed to favor redheads' son," Mr. Smith said, poking the football jock with his elbow.

"Heh, yeah, I always did," Danny replied slyly, stretching his long legs out in front of himself. "I always did. Man, I noticed her when we came in."

As Danny spoke he turned his face away from the receptionist, lest he get caught staring and looked down at his sneakers, stretching his long legs out in front of himself, crossing them over at the ankles.

"I still can't believe I got that football scholarship Dad," Danny said. "I just wish it was for a college here in our city."

"Which is why I want to make sure you get a more than thorough examination Danny," Mr. Smith said. "Once you're at that college you have no idea what the doctors there will be like. I will make sure that Doctor Rack takes good care of you."

Mr. Smith looked at his son's profile and his heart swelled with love and pride for the young man...

Danny was Mr. Smith's and his wife's only child, their pride and joy. Looking at the handsome young man sitting next to him Mr. Smith could not believe that he'd been blessed with such a handsome son, giving credit to his beautiful wife for Danny's looks but crediting himself for his more than muscular build. Mr. Smith had seen the way the receptionist looked at his son when they had arrived at the doctor's office, although Danny, being rather on the shy side didn't, or just chose not to notice. The young man was just shy of six feet tall, his body was well toned and muscular from having had played football all throughout his high school years and working out every day with weights on a regular basis. More often than not Danny's father was there at the gym to see his handsome son through the rigorous workouts, practically forcing the kid to workout till he thought he would drop from exhaustion. Danny had come to realize that his father was living out his own fantasy of being a professional football player through his son, a dream that he'd never fulfilled for himself. When Danny had come to realize that truth he at first resented his dad for it, but then, as time went on he realized that he loved football, so he didn't mind living out his father's dream. Sometimes Danny's high school buddies would be at the gym after school and see just how Danny's father would force and push the kid through the grueling workouts. How many times his buddies watched as Danny stood there sweating, grunting, shirtless because he was more than worked over as his dad shouted, "One more Son, come on, one fucking more!" Danny standing there or laying on a weight bench lifting, hefting, hoisting weights that seemed to grow heavier and heavier. How many times his buddies saw him in the locker room practically gasping for breath as he sat there with barely enough energy to get his shorts and socks off before showering. And then there were the times in the garage outside the house when Danny's father would force the young jock to hold four full gallons of paint, two in each hand out at arm's length. Danny would stand wearing just his underpants with his eyes squeezed halfway shut, his teeth clenched and the muscles in his arms and shoulders bulging as his dad would whap his butt and the backs of his thighs with a leather belt, harder than hard. The rule was that Danny had to hold the paint cans out at arm's length till his butt and thighs had been dealt at least fifty hard swats each. As Danny said, "Dad, *please,*" over and over his dad told him how proud of him he was, how this was building his body, his mind, his manly stamina and his endurance. But after all the football playing and after all the workouts Danny had attained the body of a god. Sometimes as his dad worked him out hard he would see his buddies looking at him enviously, jealously, *even lustfully?* Any artist, photographer or sculptor would have given their eyeteeth to have the strapping, young football jock model for them. Danny had the handsomest of faces, deep brown eyes, a thick handsome nose and a smile that could melt ice. Like most football players he had shoulders as broad as a doorway, stomach muscles as tight as knotted rope, big meaty hands that could palm a football, long muscular arms and a chest that would be called barrel like. When he'd been awarded the football scholarship to an out of Town College no one was more surprised than Danny himself was. His coach, his teammates and even his dad had constantly told the young robust football player just how outstanding a player he was. But it seemed that only Danny didn't believe it. He had it all it seemed; looks, an athletic build, he was a superb student and football player, yet the young jock seemed to lack in self-confidence for some reason or another. His high school had won all but one game in his last year there as a senior student. He would never forget the day his team won the championship and how a few of his teammates had carried him off the field on their shoulders, his mom and dad watching from the bleachers. They had carried him all the way into the locker room where he was showered with champagne, hoisted on various teammates shoulders and carried around the locker room like a king and patted and slapped on the butt more times than he could count. As Danny thought about that day his cock grew semi hard in his jeans. As Danny thought about all the workouts his dad had forced him through his cock grew more than semi hard in his jeans.

"Uh, Mr. Smith, Dan Smith," the red headed receptionist called out to Danny and his dad, cutting off Danny's locker room thoughts as the young man sat in Doctor Rack's waiting room.

"Uh, yeah, that's me," Danny said and stood up, the receptionist pointing at a door leading to the medical office.

"Right through there, first room on the left hand side of the hallway," the receptionist said, smiling at the young jock. "The nurse is waiting for you."

"THz-thank you," Danny said feeling more than self-conscious as his dad followed him toward the door. "My, uh, my dad wants to come with me, if that's okay."

"It's okay," the receptionist replied, still smiling widely at the young jock, seeming to be drinking in the sight of him as he passed by her work area.

"Man oh man Danny, she really likes you," Danny's father said softly as they walked toward the examining room they had been directed to.

"Yeah, but what of it?" Danny replied in question. "You thinking I should ask her out or something? Forget it. I'll be leaving for college in less than a week. No use in starting up something that I won't be able to finish."

"Who says you have to finish it Danny?" his father asked him lustfully. "Fuck man, did you see the way she was looking at your chest and shoulders nearly bulging out of your shirt? She was bulging in her panties I bet Son."

"Right in here please," a twenty something year old dark haired male nurse said, pointing at the opened door of the examining room.

Danny and his dad entered the room, the nurse holding the file in his hands. The nurse was clad in loose fitting white pants and a matching white pullover shirt with two pockets on the front of it, the standard uniform for a male nurse. Around his neck hung a stethoscope.

"Which one of you is Dan Smith?" the nurse asked, looking at the file and then looking up at the two men.

"I am," Danny replied. "This is my dad."

Without questioning why the older man was there the nurse simply pointed at the long cushioned examining table.

"Okay, strip down to your underpants and then sit up on the table please," the nurse said, putting Danny's file down on a table set up with all sorts of medical devices atop it. "From what I see written on this chart you're here for a complete medical work-up."

"Yeah, that's correct," Danny said.

As Danny shucked off his shirt, tee shirt and sneakers the nurse set up the blood pressure device next to table that he had instructed the young jock to sit on. Danny piled his clothes neatly on an extra chair, looking uncomfortably at his father at the fact that this obviously gay male nurse would see him in just his underpants. If Mr. Smith noticed his son's discomfort he made no mention of it whatsoever... What Mr. Smith was most concerned with was the examination his son was to receive, not the way his son felt at being uncomfortable for whatever the reason...

Minutes later Danny was stripped to his frosty white Calvin Klein briefs. He noticed how the male nurse seemed to drink in the sight of his smooth muscular, well-toned football player body, looking especially at his massive chest and fleshy nipples, stealing glances at the jock's slight bulge in his briefs.

"Right up here please, have a seat," the nurse said, again indicating the examination table.

"Yeah, sure," the young jock said and hoisted himself up onto the table, leaning back on the propped up upper part of it, his long legs dangling off the end of it, his bare feet just inches above the floor.

"Please extend your right arm," the nurse said, taking the blood pressure cuff in hand.

Danny did as the nurse instructed and the cuff was then wrapped tighter than tight around his upper arm. The nurse slid his stethoscope under the cuff and with his other hand pumped up the cuff with the squeeze device. Danny grimaced slightly from the pain as the tight cuff bit hard into his well-muscled arm.

"Just a few more seconds," the nurse said consolingly. "I know it hurts a bit."

"I can take it," Danny said, catching the nurse glancing at his crotch as he sat there feeling real vulnerable.

"How's my boy's blood pressure there Nurse?" Danny's father asked, sounding real brusque.

"One twenty over eighty," the nurse replied and then relieved the pressure on the cuff. "Perfect actually."

Danny breathed a soft sigh of relief as the pressure on the cuff was alleviated.

Next, the male nurse produced a disposable thermometer from one of his shirt pockets.

"Under your tongue please Mr. Smith," he said, holding up the device.

Danny opened his mouth and allowed the nurse to slide the thermometer under his tongue. For the briefest of seconds the nurse's fingertips connected with Danny's lips. He dutifully closed his mouth while the device did its work.

"Okay, that'll take a few moments, we'll make sure you're not running a fever of any kind and then Doctor Rack will be with you shortly," the nurse said, standing very close to Danny as his temperature was taken.

Danny simply nodded, his lips pursed tightly together as the thermometer in his mouth measured his temperature.

"My son here is going to be a famous football player," Mr. Smith said to the male nurse, sidling up to the other side of the table that Danny was seated on.

Danny rolled his eyes in disbelief and embarrassment as he sat there in just his underpants and his dad spoke to the nurse.

"Is that so?" the nurse asked.

"Sure as shit," Mr. Smith went on, palming a strong hand against the back of his son's bull-like neck. "He won a scholarship from his high school and he's on his way to a college out of town to play football. Man, I will bet that in no time my boy here will be the college football captain."

"Well, I'm sure you're correct Mr. Smith," the nurse said, giving Danny's shoulder a squeeze. "He sure is built for it."

As Danny was about to give the nurse a mean look and to tell him to get his hands off him the nurse chose that moment to take the thermometer out of the football jock's mouth. He slid it out slowly, caressing Danny's pursed lips with it, it seemed. He examined the thermometer as Danny looked at him angrily and Danny's father held his hand against his son's neck.

"Any fever?" Danny asked sarcastically.

"No, you're at ninety eight point seven," the nurse said and tossed the disposable thermometer in a trash bucket. "Perfectly normal."

"Glad to hear that," Mr. Smith said, moving his hand up and ruffling his son's hair. "Wouldn't want my boy headed off to college with a fever or anything like that."

"Okay, Mr. Smith, please help me get your son here secured to the table and then I'll let Doctor Rack know that he's ready to be examined," the nurse said, reaching under the table and producing a short leather restraint-like strap. "There's a matching strap like this one at your side of the table as well."

"Uh, yeah, sure," Mr. Smith said, reaching under the table and finding the device that the nurse had indicated.

"Sec-secured to the table?" Danny said, suddenly sounding very nervous as the nurse quickly and efficiently locked his wrist into the restraint, securing Danny's hand against the lower side of the table. "Wh-what's this all about man?"

Danny turned to his father at the other side of the table and saw that he, like the nurse was getting his other wrist secured to the side of the table as well.

"Wh-why are you tyin' me up like this for?" Danny asked the nurse, again looking in his direction, but the nurse moving to the foot end of the table.

"Doctor Rack's orders Sir," the nurse replied, but looking at Danny's father. "The doctor likes his patients to be totally secured to the table during an intense examination. He doesn't want to risk the patient falling from the table or accidentally moving while giving an injection or while administering a blood test."

"I guess that sounds reasonable huh Danny?" the jocks father asked him with a grin and turning his attention back to the nurse.

"Mr. Smith, I'll need to secure your feet as well and get the end of the table raised," the nurse said to Danny and again turned to the older man. "I'll have to ask you to remove your son's underpants for him Mr. Smith."

"Hey now hold on there," the muscular restrained jock chirped a tad more than nervously at that point. "You said for me to strip down to my underpants."

"That was for the blood test and temperature part of the exam, my part of the exam," the nurse explained. "This is for Doctor Rack's part of the exam."

"It's doctor's orders son," Mr. Smith said and stepped up to the table, placing his hands on the sides of Danny's briefs.

"Oh jeez Dad," the muscle boy whispered, not wanting to mention that he had just laid a massive hard-on a few seconds ago.

Danny watched with a tight grimace on his handsome face as his father slid his underpants off him, his erect cock springing up between his muscular tree-trunk like thighs, his big juicy peach fuzzed balls landing on the cushioned table. Danny got a nose full of the scent emanating from his sweaty and juicy balls and he wondered if the nurse and his dad could smell them too.

"Looks like that pretty receptionist out there really did get you going huh Danny?" his father asked him, indicating his hard-on.

"Dad, please," Danny whispered and watched then as the nurse squatted in front of him and worked at getting his ankles secured in the restraints at the foot end of the table.

The nurse took his time about getting the jock's ankles secured in the restraints. Danny noticed how the guy seemed to be enjoying holding his beefy feet in hand before locking them into the ankle restraints. Once Danny's ankles were locked in the restraints the nurse used a lever under the table to push the end of the table upwards so that Danny's feet were spread wide and his hole was embarrassingly on display.

"Are you sure all of this is part of the examination that the doctor wants to do on my boy?" Danny's father asked the nurse, still holding his son's underpants in his hand.

"Totally positive Mr. Smith," the nurse replied. "As a matter of fact Doctor Rack insists upon it. This makes it all the easier for him to examine his patient."

Danny looked miserably at his father, feeling like a tied down Thanksgiving turkey all spread out on the table.

"Okay, I'm done here," the nurse said, stepping next to Danny for a moment. "I'll leave you two for now and Doctor Rack will be in very shortly."

"Thank you Nurse thanks a lot," Danny's father said.

"I hope your examination goes well Mr. Smith," the nurse said to Danny and gave one of his nipples a fast squeeze, then scurried out of the examination lab.

"H-hey," Danny said to the nurse's back as a droplet of pre cum oozed from his wide sexy slit and slid down the shaft of his hard beefy penis.

Danny looked angrily at his father as the older man placed his son's underpants on the stack of his clothes.

"Did you see that shit Dad?" Danny asked his father through clenched teeth. "Did you see what the fuck he just did? That faggot squeezed my damned man tit!!"

"Yeah, I saw that, maybe we should report that to the doc when he gets in here," Mr. Smith said, stepping over to the table. "It's more than obvious that like me you've got really sensitive nipples there."

That said and with a grin on his face Mr. Smith gave his son's left nipple a fast twist.

"Dad please," Danny laughed along with his father, trying to mask his feeling of foreboding and apprehension at the examination that he was about to endure. "Dad, take the straps off me, *please man. God, look at me here, fucking stripped naked and tied to a damned table!"*

"It's doctor's orders Son, and you really don't have anything to worry about," Mr. Smith said reassuringly. "I'll be right here the whole time."

"Jeez, that's what I'm afraid of," Danny whispered, leaning his head back on the table as his father again twisted one of his nipples.

"You know, I never noticed before but your nipples are as fleshy as your mothers," Danny's father said and again squeezed and twisted his son's nipple, causing more pre cum to ooze from his slit. "Yeah, heh, heh, as sensitive as mine and as fleshy as your mothers. You know, your mother's tits were one of the reasons I fell in love with her, or should I say, two of the reasons."

Laughing, Danny's father reached across his son's chest and gave his other nipple a good squeeze and a twist.

"This one just as sensitive?" Mr. Smith asked his son, Danny's nipple squeezed tight between his first two fingers and his thumb, jiggling it.

"Dad," Danny whispered. "Stop this please…leave my damned man tits alone!"

"What's the matter son?" Danny's father asked him jovially. "I'm your dad here; I'm just having some fun with my boy. Yeah, even during the workouts when you had your shirt off I never noticed just how meaty and fleshy your man tits were."

Danny gulped hard and oozed more pre cum as his dad squeezed and really twisted the tar out of his nipple.

"And just like me you call 'em your man tits," Mr. Smith said, again taking his son's other nipple back in his fingers and thumb. "Who knows when you heard me call 'em that, but I always did. Never wanted to refer to my nipples as just tits that would make me sound like a woman."

Danny simply smiled at his father and tried to laugh along with the older man as he tweaked and squeezed his nipples.

"Grrrrrrrr!!! *Man tits*!!!" Mr. Smith said in a growling tone, jiggling one of Danny's nipples real hard. "Feels great to have 'em worked huh Son? *Man's fucking tits*!!!"

"If, if you say so Dad," Danny replied softly.

"Hell yeah and just like me it really gets you in motion to have those man tits worked on huh son?" Mr. Smith asked Danny, letting go of his nipple and placing his thumb and first two fingers around the crown of his son's erect cock.

At his father's touch on his most private area Danny gasped loudly.

"HuHHH...D-dad..." Danny whispered, watching in bewilderment as his dad ran the pad of his thumb over his pre cum slicked wide slit.

"Yep, just like your dear old dad here, really gets you going to have your man tits worked on," Mr. Smith said and let go of his son's beefy hard cock. "I just hope that someday you find a girl who knows how to appreciate those man tits of yours Danny."

"Y-yeah, me too," Danny replied, thanking God that his dad had let go of his cock, feeling that he was about to shoot a load of jock boy juice if he hadn't let go.

Just then the door to the examination lab opened and a middle aged man of average height with thinning brown hair and wire rim glasses entered the room.

"Good day, good day, I am Doctor Rack," the sinister looking man said as he entered the room, closing the door behind him.

He was clad in the traditional long white doctor's smock with a shirt and tie under it, a stethoscope dangling around his wiry looking neck. He walked over to the table where the nurse had left Danny's chart followed by Danny's father, seemingly oblivious of the young muscle boy strapped up to the examining table. He picked up the chart and looked at Mr. Smith.

"Are you Dan Smith?" Doctor Rack asked Danny's father.

"Uh, no Sir, I'm Dan Smith's father," Mr. Smith said replied, shaking the doctor's hand and quickly letting go. "That's my boy over there on your examining table."

Doctor Rack looked over at the strapped up muscle jock and smiled broadly.

"Ah, good, good, this makes more sense now," the doctor said happily. "For a moment there I thought I was going to have to fire my nurse. He knows the rules after all. All patients are to be secured in before I get to them. Makes my job of examination that much easier."

"Yeah, so the nurse said," Mr. Smith said as Doctor Rack seemed to be drinking in the sight of Danny.

"So, you are Dan Smith," Doctor Rack said, looking at the muscular handsome jock. "Yeah, that uh, that's me," Danny responded, sounding nervous feeling totally self-conscious at the fact that his cock was harder than hard, more erect than erect.

"And I see that according to your chart that your father here has brought you to me for a full medical work-up for your college scholarship," the doctor went on.

"Yeah, that's right," Danny said.

"Uh Doc, I hope you don't mind that I want to be here while you examine my boy," Mr. Smith said, standing behind the doctor. "I just want to make sure he gets a real thorough examination."

"No, no, not at all, it's your prerogative, he's your son," the doctor said, turning around to look at Mr. Smith. "As a matter of fact you can most likely assist me in certain areas of the examination."

"Sounds good to me," Mr. Smith said. "Where do we start?"

"Well, I'll need to take his temperature before we do anything," Doctor Rack said, glancing at the strapped to the table muscle boy.

"Your nurse already took my temperature," Danny piped up. "And there was something else he did that needs to be mentioned here..."

"My nurse took your temperature orally," Doctor Rack said, sounding rather stern all of a sudden, cutting off Danny's words in mid-sentence. "I am going to take it rectal fashion."

Danny gulped hard, looking sheepishly at his dad and mouthing the words "Holy shit" as the doctor opened a drawer and produced two jars marked "Lubricant." He handed one of the jars to Danny's father.

"You've got to be kidding," Danny said softly as the two men approached the table.

Danny thought that for sure that if he wasn't strapped to the table that he would have bolted out of the room for sure…

"Okay, we'll need to get your son's rectum good and lubricated, seeing as the thermometer I use is rather awkward in size," Doctor Rack explained to Mr. Smith, taking the lid off his jar, his father following suit.

"Aw-*awkward in size?*" Danny squeaked, looking beseechingly at his father to tell this doctor to stop, to stop this instant.

But instead the two men opened their jars of lubricant and suddenly the smell of peppermint seemed to fill the air around the examination table.

"What is that stuff Doc?" Danny asked.

"Just a peppermint scented lubricant to make it easier for me to take your temperature young man," Doctor Rack said, dipping three of his fingers into the jar. "It is mixed with vitamins, herbs and some strong supplements as well. Mr. Smith, I'll lubricate your son's rectum first and then you can give him a helping from your jar. I suggest that we each lubricate him three to five times. I want to insure that he's soft and moist in there to take my thermometer when I'm ready to take his temperature."

"Sure thing Doc," Mr. Smith said, watching as Doctor Rack stepped between Danny's spread legs and slid his three slicked fingers into his son's gaping ass hole, hefting the jock's juicy balls out of the way with his other hand.

"OHHH G-GOD," Danny suddenly blubbered breathlessly, his massively muscular chest arching straight up, his tweaked up nipples jutting straight out. "Oh God Dad, this guy has got me by the balls…"

"Relax Son, let the doc do his work," Mr. Smith said, dipping his fingers into his jar of peppermint scented lubricant. "MMM, this stuff really smells good huh, Danny?"

"Y-yeah, sure thing Dad," Danny replied, squirming miserably atop the table as Doctor Rack slid his fingers deeper into Danny's hole, moistening up the sides of it inwardly. "If you say so Dad, sm-smells great…"

The scent of Danny's sweaty balls mixed with the lubricant wafted up to his nostrils and caused a thrilling sensation to course through his very being. He oozed more pre cum from his slit as he felt Doctor Rack giving his peach fuzzed sweaty balls a slight squeeze. Danny's mind was reeling and he wondered if all football players had to endure this kind of examination.

"OHHH good God," Danny whispered and heaved his chest back down to the table.

"I know it's uncomfortable son," Doctor Rack said sympathetically, sliding his fingers all over the inside of Danny's hole, really prodding him like crazy. "But I assure you it's very important for the examination."

"If, if you say so Doc," Danny said and then Doctor Rack slid his fingers slowly out of Danny's hole, letting go of his balls as well.

Danny felt a moment of relief once his hole was free of the doctor's fingers, but then, not wasting any time his father slid his three lubricant slicked fingers into his son's hole.

"UHHHnnn," Danny gasped and again arched his chest up off the table. "Ea-easy Dad, you've got thick fingers there."

Like the Doctor Danny's father burrowed his fingers deep into his son's hole, really getting him good and lubricated, holding his balls up and out of the way just as the doctor had done as well. As the lubricant coated his hole and the rosebud of his ass Danny felt his cock tingling, throbbing. Actually the muscular jock was starting to feel hornier with each passing second.

"HMMM, looks like I'll have to restrain your son's upper torso Mr. Smith," Doctor Rack said to Danny's father, watching as the young man heaved his chest up and down on the table as his father prodded and poked his ass hole. "I insist that my patients be totally still during an examination."

Danny was breathless as the doctor stepped next to him and produced a long strap from under the table.

"Chest down please young man," Doctor Rack said to Danny and brazenly gave one of the jock's erect hard nipples a squeeze.

"F-fuck, wh-what is it with all of you in this place and my damned man tits?" Danny gasped and slowly lowered his massive chest back down to the table.

The young man felt miserable as the doc laid the strap just under his mammoth-like male cleavage and pulled it tight, securing Danny's upper body now to the table as well.

"UHHHrrrrr, UHHHrrrrrrr, UHHHrrrrr, fuck," Danny garbled as his dad slid his fingers out of his hole and let go of his balls.

"Easy son, no swearing in front of the doc here," Danny's father admonished him.

"No, no, it's perfectly all right, I assure you," the doctor said with a sinister looking smile. "I am sure he is most uncomfortable. If a little swearing helps get him through it all so be it."

"Your turn Doc," Mr. Smith said, holding up his fingers. "I'm dried up here for the moment."

"Yes, yes, so you are," Doctor Rack said, picking up his jar of lubricant, stepping to the front of the table and dipping four of his fingers this time into the gooey stuff.

Danny watched; a feeling of helplessness engulfing him as the doc really got his fingers smeared with the stuff a second time.

"Try to relax now son," Doctor Rack then said and slowly slid his four fingers into Danny's rectum, taking the jock's balls again in his other hand and hefting them up and out of the way, squeezing them every few seconds.

"UHHH..." Danny groaned and this time when he tried to arch his chest up the heavy strap held him in check and he felt a strong chilling and numbing sensation in his chest and nipples (man tits.)

"There you go Danny boy, you're doing great," Mr. Smith said and to Danny's shock his father took his erect cock in hand.

"Boy oh boy Danny, you're throbbing like the world's greatest lover here," the jock's father said, giving his hardness a few tugs. "You haven't gone down once since we got in here."

Danny oozed pre cum like crazy and looked at his father in total wonderment and awe.

"D-dad, pl-please, let go of my cock," Danny grumbled.

"Hey relax Son," Mr. Smith said with a wide grin, tightening his grip on the jock's cock as the doctor's fingers prodded his hole deeper and deeper; his other hand giving his balls squeezes more than every few seconds. "I'm just trying to get you through this exam. God knows it must be real uncomfortable having the doc's fingers jammed in your hole."

"Uncomfortable isn't the word," Danny mumbled, feeling totally humiliated at that point.

Mr. Smith let go of his son's erection, and just in time Danny thought, seeing as he felt he was about to shoot that pent-up load of jock boy soup. How humiliating would that have been the kid thought, to shoot his load in front of his old man and the doctor here? Alas, poor Danny had no clue of just how much he was in for, and shooting his load would have been a good consolation actually...

"Say Doctor Rack," Danny said breathlessly, looking down at the doctor as his four fingers wiggled around and around in his hole, lubricating him more and more. "I-I'm feeling real funny here man! Actually, to put it plainly and bluntly I'm feeling real fucking horny and sleazy."

"That's my boy!!" Danny's father said proudly.

"The lubricant that I am moistening your rectum with is as I said mixed with herbs and vitamins," the doctor explained, greasing up the walls of Danny's hole more and more. "Other patients of mine have said the same thing that it seemed to stimulate them in that way. Nothing to worry about Son. It's perfectly normal what you're feeling."

But what Danny really wanted to say was that he felt like shooting his load... Actually the jock felt like he could shoot a load big enough to choke a horse...and then some.

"Y-you mean that that lubricant acts as a sort of aphrodisiac?" Danny asked breathlessly.

"Yes, you might put it that way," the doctor replied, burrowing his fingers still deeper into the muscular jock's hole, wiggling his fingers against the walls of it in there.

"J-jeez, and that stuff is getting into my bloodstream as well?" Danny asked sounding sort of scared. "Th-that's why I'm feelin' so worked up?"

"Nothing to worry about Son," Doctor Rack said reassuringly, slowly extracting his fingers from the jock's hole. "It's perfectly harmless."

A few minutes later it was again Danny's father's turn to lubricate his son's hole. Standing in front of his handsome strapped up son the older man slid his slicked four fingers into Danny's sopped up hole.

"UHHHnnnn, G-God, this is the fourth time," Danny garbled, his head spinning.

At that point Danny was starting to sweat atop the table. His father thrust his fingers in really deep, causing the jock some pain.

"H-hey Dad, t-take it easy huh?" Danny asked miserably. "L-like I said you've got pretty thick fingers after all."

"Heh, you can take it Son, I built you stronger than that," Mr. Smith said, hefting his son's peach fuzzed balls up, squeezing them. "You should see the workouts I put this kid through on a daily basis Doc. Don't you think for a blasted moment that he achieved that muscular body all on his own. I put my boy here through hell so that he can look the way he does."

"You're a good father Mr. Smith," Doctor Rack said, standing next to Danny, giving one of the jock's nipples a squeeze and twist.

"Fuck, this is the craziest examination I've ever had," the jock said, watching as his own dad thrust his fingers in and out of his hole, his cock doing a throb dance and twitching now between his legs.

The sounds of squishing seemed to be filling the room at that point. Danny's hole was that sopped, that lubricated by that time. Yet when his father slid his fingers out of his hole Doctor Rack again dipped his fingers into his jar of lubricant and rather anxiously slid them far into the jock's waiting hole.

"OHHH j-jeez," Danny blubbered. "J-just take my temperature already."

"Soon young man, very soon," the doctor said, hefting Danny's peach fuzzed balls up as he slid his fingers deep into the jock's hole.

"G-God, I feel like some cheap faggot whore on a Saturday night the way you two are fingerin' the tar outa me," Danny mumbled to his father as the older man stood at his son's side. "C-can't help bein' so hard and erect here Doc. Y-you got me by the balls after all."

Doctor Rack simply grinned at the young man and thrust his fingers in and out of the jock's hole, practically touching his prostate deep within. It seemed like this time that the doc was taking his sweet time about it. Actually it seemed that this time he didn't want to take his fingers from Danny's hole. With his mouth hanging agape Danny turned his head to look at his father.

"You're doing great Son," his father said and again took the jock's erection in his hand. "And look at this shit Doc, my boy here *is still* hard as a fucking rock."

Danny's cock oozed a thick pearl of pre cum as his dad held it straight out for Doctor Rack to see.

"Yes, so I see," the doctor said and finally slid his fingers out of Danny's hole.

"Yeah, I guess that pretty receptionist of yours out front really has my kid in a lather here," Mr. Smith laughed, giving Danny's hard cock a few pulls.

"OHHHrrrrr D-dad," Danny gasped and almost shot his load, but his father again let go of him just in time.

"Mr. Smith?" Doctor Rack said pointing at Danny's waiting hole with his greasy looking index finger.

"Yeah, sure thing Doc," Danny's father said and dipped his fingers into his jar of lubricant again.

Breathing in short gasps, his cock twitching and hard Danny watched as his dad again slid his fingers into his gaping hole...

By the time they were done Danny's father and Doctor Rack had lubricated Danny's hole more than five times each. He was beyond sopped, to the point that he felt the lubricant oozing from his hole and landing on the table he was strapped up to. The scent of peppermint wafted all over the room, but mostly from the poor jock's moist hole.

"Okay now, I think that we are ready to take your temperature Danny," the doctor said, opening a middle drawer on a medical cabinet.

He rummaged through the drawer and then looked at Danny and his father apologetically.

"I'm so sorry, I must have left the thermometer in the other room in the sterilizing liquid," Doctor Rack said, stepping to the door of the examination room. "I'll just run and get it. I won't be more than a couple of moments. In the meantime I'll send the nurse in to clean the part of the table where the lubricant is dripping."

"B-but," Danny blubbered as Doctor Rack left the room quickly, closing the door behind him. "But that nurse is a faggot!! Oh God Dad, please, take the straps off me man!!"

"Now I don't have to tell you again Danny, its Doctor Rack's orders that you be secured in for the examination," Mr. Smith reminded his son, ruffling his short hair. "Can't tell you how proud I am of you today Danny boy. I mean, my son, being examined by a top of the line doctor because he won a football scholarship!"

"Jeez, I wonder if that exec who left here earlier was strapped up like I am right now," Danny said wonderingly to his father. "Fuck, strapped up with his hole all smeared with that candy smelling goop that you and the doc worked into *my* hole. What do you think?"

"I would think he was," Danny's father replied. "I mean why would the doc have you strapped up for an exam and not that guy? And you heard the great things that that suit guy said about Doctor Rack before he left here."

"Yeah, sure," Danny said with a grin. "Jeez, all those suit guys wear knee length dark colored dress socks Dad. I've heard that from buddies of mine in school about their executive dads. Ha, bet Doctor Rack had that suit guy strapped to the table with his long socks on, ha, ha, only because it would have taken too long for the guy to get 'em off, ha, ha, ha!!!"

Danny's dad laughed along with him while the jock's hard cock did a twitching dance again as he thought about the executive strapped down in his long socks… He wondered then how many times the doc had smeared that handsome executive's hole with that peppermint smelling lubricant.

"But fuck it all Dad, that slop that you and the doc smeared in my hole really is makin' me hornier than a bitch in heat," Danny mused.

Just then the door to the examining room opened and the male nurse walked in, holding a sterile white cloth.

"Okay, Doctor Rack says you're ready for your anal temperature," the nurse said, stepping up to the front of the table and wiping the lubricant that had dripped from the jock's hole from the tabletop."

"Yeah, yeah, I guess I am at that," Danny said, seeing as the nurse was looking intently at his sopped hole. "Wow, looks like Doctor Rack really got you more than lubricated," the nurse said with a grin and to Danny's shock slid two finger's into the jock's hole. "Yep, he did a great job in here."

"Hey, get your fingers out of my damned shit chute man," Danny snapped at the nurse.

"Usually Doctor Rack will have me lube up the patient while they're waiting for him," the nurse said, sliding his fingers deeper into Danny's sopped crevice, getting a good hearty grunt out of the strapped down jock boy.

"G-get your fingers out of my hole I said," Danny gasped through clenched teeth.

The nurse simply did as he was told and left the room.

"God almighty Dad, did you see that shit?" Danny asked his dad more than angrily now. "That fucking Homo faggot tweaked my hole!"

"Yeah I did see that Danny," Mr. Smith said, sounding not at all angry. "Maybe we'd better tell the doc about that too, when we tell him how that nurse also gave one of your man tits a squeeze earlier."

Smiling devilishly Danny's father grabbed his son's nipples, hard.

"OWWW!!" Danny barked as his dad squeezed and twisted his nipples.

"Fuck man, better tits than your mother Danny," Mr. Smith said and yanked hard on his son's nipples. "Fuck it all, you should get a couple of girls to really work the hell outa these nubs for you!!"

That said, Danny's father again let go of his son's nipples and Danny's cock throbbed mightily, pre cum oozing from it like crazy now. His strapped up chest was awash with chills and thrills, his nipples tingling like two vibrating cherries on his massive chest. Then, the door to the exam room opened and Doctor Rack walked back in, holding the rectal thermometer in hand…

"Okay then, here we are," the doctor said cheerily, closing the door behind him, holding an over-sized thermometer in his hand.

"Th-that's the thermometer?" Danny asked, nearly in a panic when he saw the size of the device.

It looked to Danny like some over-sized dildo that one would purchase in a kinky sex shop. It was at least eight to nine inches in length and looked to be as thick as a ripe cucumber. Danny saw that there were numbers and thin lines etched along the device and a switch was embedded to the bottom of it.

"Y-you can't be serious about using that thing to take my temperature with Doc," Danny babbled as the doctor stepped to the front of the table between Danny's legs.

"Well now you see why I had to have you so thoroughly lubricated young man," Doctor Rack said. "Mr. Smith, if you would assist me again I will be more than grateful. Usually my nurse assists in these matters but seeing as I have you here…"

"Sure thing Doc, what can I do for you?" Danny's father asked, stepping next to Doctor Rack, cutting the doctor off in mid-sentence.

"Under the table, just under your son's legs is a turning lever," the doctor said. "Please reach under there and turn it until your son's legs are spread apart. It will make it easier for him when I insert the thermometer, seeing as he seems to be having misgivings about this."

"Sure thing Doc," Mr. Smith said and squatted in front of the table, his face mere inches from his son's sopping wet hole.

Danny's father grabbed the lever and began turning it in a clockwise direction, Danny's legs being slowly spread wide, his gaping hole becoming more and more visible with each turn.

"Oh God, oh jeez, *Dad, stop,*" the muscled jock begged, looking in horror at the thermometer in the doctor's hand and feeling more and more humiliated as his most private sector was being put on display.

"Now Danny, I don't want to have to tell you again about doctor's orders!!" Danny's father said sternly, glancing up at his son for a moment.

The look of anguish on his son's face nearly tore the older man's heart out but then he remembered that all this was being done for his own well-being.

"MMM, the scent of peppermint down here is really strong Doc," Danny's father commented, his nose and mouth less than a few inches from his son's widely splayed hole. "Looks like we really did lube my kid up real well after all."

"Indeed we did," the doctor said.

"Heh smells almost good enough to eat Doc," Mr. Smith laughed, finished turning the lever to get his son's legs spread.

"Actually it is edible," the doctor said, quickly stepping next to his patient and tying a black cloth over the jock's eyes.

"H-hey, wh-what are you doin' now, *blindfolding me*???" Danny chirped nervously, and then to his utter horror felt what he was sure was a tongue flicking around in his spread hole. "HuHHH!!!

D-dad, oh jeez dad, I sure as hell hope that isn't you down there…*oh Gods…I-I bet it's that faggot male nurse! Wh-what are you thinkin' Doc, lettin' that perv eat my hole…"*

In the next second Danny smelled a strange odor. It swirled under his nostrils and into his mouth and as the sensations of his hole being eaten and slurped at some more his rock hard cock did a twitching dance between his splayed out legs.

"OHHH, wh-what's happening here?" Danny murmured and his head seemed to spin away.

He felt large hands (*his father's hands???*) caressing the walls of his butt cheeks and the tongue that was working its magic in his hole flicked faster and with total determination.

"OHHH f-fuck, s-someone's eatin' my shit chute Dad," Danny murmured in the state of dizzy ecstasy that he found himself spinning in.

When he opened his eyes the blindfold was gone, as if it had never been there. He wondered if it had been there at all… He looked straight ahead and saw Doctor Rack again standing between his splayed legs, holding the over-sized thermometer in hand.

"Wh-what happened?" Danny croaked.

"You must have dozed off for a moment young man," Doctor Rack said. "Perfectly normal under the circumstances."

"Wh-where's my dad?" Danny asked as the doctor began slowly inserting the thermometer into the jock's rectum.

"He stepped out to use the lavatory," the doctor replied. "Now just relax…"

"OHHH, OHHH j-jeez Doc," Danny moaned as the plastic device made its way inside him.

"You're doing fine so far," Doctor Rack said and slid the device further into Danny's sopped hole.

"UHHHnnn," the jock breathed heavily, leaning his head back and looking up at the ceiling. "G-God, now I know why you needed to have me strapped up to the table and why you needed to really get my shit chute lubricated the way you did…"

"Right you are young man," Doctor Rack said, sliding the thermometer all the way into Danny's hole until just the switch at the bottom of it was visible.

Danny could have sworn that he felt the walls of his hole sucking the device in, and as they did his hardness throbbed between his legs. He wondered how strange it would sound to ask the doc to somehow get him off, but quickly changed his mind as the doctor placed the tip of a finger against the switch on the bottom of the over-sized thermometer.

"I do hope you're not too uncomfortable Danny," the doctor said, sounding concerned.

"N, no, s-so far I think I'm okay," the muscled jock replied, trying to sound as brave as possible, but feeling more than miserable and humiliated.

The jock felt as if his hole had been stretched to epic lengths as the invasive thermometer tormented him…

"Okay then, you're now going to hear a buzzing sound and you may feel a vibrating sensation in your anus," the doctor said and flicked the switch up on the thermometer in Danny's hole.

Suddenly and all at once the well-muscled jock felt more than a vibrating sensation in his hole, he felt what to him was a swarm of bees buzzing around deep inside him.

"OHHH, aHHH *j-jeez Doc,*" Danny chirruped and gulped hard. "It, it feels like a damned woman's vibrator you got wedged in me!"

Heh, that is an interesting way of putting it," the doctor remarked.

The jock squirmed miserably under the tight binding straps as the doctor stepped next to the table.

"Just try to relax young man," the doctor said reassuringly, ruffling the jock's hair and giving one of his nipples a really hard twist.

Danny simply looked at the doctor with an expression of aghast.

"Fuckin' dudes here love my man tits," the muscle boy murmured and pursed his lips tightly together.

Doctor Rack then reached under the table, took another lever in hand and began slowly turning it. To Danny's dismay the table he was strapped up to began moving backward, stretching him out like a tight side of beef.

"H-hey, wh-what are you doin' now Doc?" Danny asked, sounding confused as he turned his head from side to side, looking at the sides of the table.

The sounds of the thermometer buzzing in his hole seemed to grow louder and fill the air around him.

"Just preparing you for the next phase of the exam young man," Doctor Rack replied, turning the lever some more. "Usually my nurse handles these matters…"

"N-no, not the nurse Doc," Danny remarked and then found himself in a very awkward and humiliating position.

His upper muscular body was lain out and stretched tight under the straps and his butt was now more than in the air while the buzzing thermometer tormented him with each passing second. His big feet dangled in the restraints, his toes curling back every few seconds.

"HuHHH, oHHHrrrr G-God," Danny panted, looking down at his pre cum oozing wide slit as it stared up at him, his cock rock hard and throbbing, his big juicy balls dangling between his spread legs just over the thermometer.

"D-doc, I-I'm feelin' more and more sleazy here man," the jock remarked. "And jeez what a fucked up position you got me in now..."

"It's necessary Danny," the doctor said, let go of the lever, gave one of the jock's nipples a squeeze and stepped to the front of the table between Danny's spread legs.

Danny watched as the doctor slid the thermometer slightly out of his hole and seemed to be examining the numbers on it. He then slid it back in only to slide it back out again, slightly further this time. He studied some more numbers and then slid the device slowly back into the jock's hole.

"OHHHH!!!" Danny moaned. "D-doc is; is that thing almost done taking my temperature?"

Doctor Rack smiled at the jock and this time slid the thermometer halfway out.

"No, unfortunately it's a slow process Danny," the doctor replied and as he slid it back in again Danny felt as if the walls of his hole were again actually sucking the thing in, greedily. "I realize how difficult this all is for you, but I assure you you're doing very well."

"HuuuuuHHH!!!" the muscle boy groaned, feeling as if he were being fucked like some cheap whore.

Danny's lips quivered and his cock throbbed harder and harder as the doctor slid the thermometer almost all the way out only to slide it back in again, wedging it good and tight in the jock's sopped hole. Danny felt the tip of the thing teasing his prostate and the walls of his hole were alive and tingling with the buzzing sensation.

"OHHH D-doc, c-can't help it, I'm feelin' more than horny and worked up here," Danny panted.

"Yes, so I can see that," the doctor replied and took the muscle boy's hardness in hand for a moment, giving it a teasing-like squeeze.

"OHHHrrrrr fuck, b-between my man tits and my hard cock you guys here are drivin' me bananas," Danny panted. "Up to and including my dad…"

"I will be examining your penis, but not at this moment Danny," Doctor Rack said and gave the muscle boy's hardness a few tugs, sending chills and thrills through his very being.

"AHHH…" Danny moaned and felt somewhat miserable when the doctor let go of his throbbing member.

"Well, I'm back guys," Danny's father said as he entered the examining room. "How's my boy doing Doc?"

"So far so good Mr. Smith," the doctor replied, turning and glancing at Danny's father.

Danny looked miserably at his father as the older man took in the sight of his stretched out son.

"Man, what is that buzzing sound?" Mr. Smith asked. "Sounds like an airplane of some sort."

"It's the thermometer that is taking your boy's temperature," Doctor Rack explained. "And I must say that so far he's enduring it all quite well. You can well imagine how uncomfortable he is right now."

"Yeah, sure looks it Doc," Danny's father said, sidling up next to the table his son was on and ruffling his sweat soaked hair.

"But my boy also knows that all this is more than a requirement if he wants to play college football."

"D-dad..." Danny whispered, looking at his father beseechingly.

"Yeah I know son, but don't worry, you'll be done soon I'm sure," Mr. Smith said.

"On the contrary Mr. Smith, I have lots more to examine where your boy here is concerned," Doctor Rack said. "Perhaps you could assist me again. I'm now going to examine Danny's feet while the thermometer finishes its work."

"Yeah, sure thing Doc," Danny's father said to Doctor Rack.

"And then after that I'll have my nurse take some blood from him," the doctor went on. "While the nurse is doing that you and I can take a coffee break."

"Yeah, that sounds good Doc," Danny said practically breathlessly. "Coffee sounds good..."

"Sorry young man, no coffee for you," the doctor said sadly, looking at Danny. "I don't want any caffeine in your bloodstream during a blood test."

Danny grimaced miserably, realizing that his little ploy to get off the table hadn't worked.

"Okay Doc, what say we take care of my boy's feet now?" Danny's father suggested. "He's gonna need them in good shape when he gets to that college to play football."

"Oh God Dad," Danny whimpered as his cock throbbed as his dad talked about his feet.

"Now Danny, let's check out those feet of yours shall we?" Doctor Rack said, taking two straight plastic stick-like devices and two jars that were marked "Foot Lotion" from another drawer.

Danny gulped hard and the thermometer wedged in his hole seemed to buzz louder and the sensations seemed to increase with each passing second.

"Wh-why don't you just send me to a foot doctor to have my damn feet checked out?" Danny whimpered as Doctor Rack handed the jock's father one of the stick-like devices and one of the jars of foot lotion.

Then Doctor Rack and Mr. Smith each pulled a stool up between Danny's spread legs and sat down.

"Why would I need to do that when I can check everything out right here in my lab?" Doctor Rack replied placing his stick-like device on the table Danny was strapped up to, right next to his tingling and cum stuffed balls; Danny's father did the same with his stick-like device. "No, no, it's much easier to examine you from top to bottom right here in my lab. That is why your dad here brought you to me after all Danny."

"Doctor's orders son," the elder Mr. Smith reminded Danny.

"Y-yeah, I suppose you're right," Danny said softly and gasped as the doctor gave the thermometer in his hole a turn. "UHHHh!!!"

"Should be done taking your temperature very soon Danny boy," the doctor said, opening the jar of foot lotion and glancing at Danny's father, gesturing for him to follow suit. "Your boy is doing very well Mr. Smith. Now, let's grease up his feet with the lotion shall we?"

"Sounds like a plan to me Doc," Danny's father replied.

Mr. Smith and the doctor dipped their fingers into the lotion and each of them applied a goodly amount of the peppermint scented stuff to the jock's feet as they twitched in the ankle restraints.

"S-say, is that the same stuff you used to lubricate my hole Doc?" the jock asked wonderingly, looking down, watching and feeling chills throughout his god-like body as the doctor and his dad massaged the lotion all over his big feet. "It sure smells like it from here."

"It's the same scent, but not the same medication Danny," Doctor Rack replied, working the lotion between Danny's toes and all over the tops and beefy bottoms of the muscle boy's foot that he was working on. "This lotion will be used to sensitize your feet so that I can and with your father's help appropriately check your reflexes."

"Ch-check my reflexes?" Danny asked, watching as his father worked the lotion all over his foot, between his toes and all over the tops and bottoms of them.

He noticed that his father seemed as enraptured by his feet as he had been by his nipples, or more appropriately, his man tits. As the lotion was being smoothed over his feet Danny felt a numbing yet tingling sensation all over the various sections of his feet. He watched as the doctor and his dad used both hands to massage the lotion against his wide arches at the same time, moving their hands over the jock's ankles.

"Almost like a pedicure huh son?" Danny's father asked him.

"Sure thing Dad, if you say so," the jock replied.

"What size are your feet Danny?" the doctor asked.

"T-ten and a half," Danny replied and gasped again as the doctor gave the thermometer in his hole another turn. "UHHHH!!! B-but you can measure them if you're not sure."

"Oh, on that I will take your word Danny," Doctor Rack replied with a fiendish looking grin.

Then, the doctor and Danny's father put the lids on the jars of foot lotion, placed the jars on Danny's table and picked up the stick-like devices.

"Okay, now let's check your son's feet reflexes," the doctor said to Mr. Smith. "This will be very important, seeing as he is planning to have a football career. Do as I do Mr. Smith."

That said, Doctor Rack took Danny's right foot by the ankle and turned it so that the bottom of the jock's beefy foot was facing him. Danny's father did the same with his left foot. Doctor Rack slid the stick-like device up and down the bottom of Danny's foot, starting at the jock's heel and working his way up. Watching what the doctor was doing Danny's father did the same thing to Danny's left foot…

"H-hey, ha, ha, ha, ha, ha, ha, ha!!!" Danny suddenly gurgled. S-say, that tickles Doc!!"

"I realize that Danny, but it's the only way for me to check your reflexes," Doctor Rack replied and moved his stick back down the bottom of Danny's foot, his father doing the same with his other foot.

"Ha, ha, ha, ha, ha, ha, ha!!!" Danny laughed.

"Are you ticklish on a normal basis?" the doctor asked and moved the stick along Danny's wide arch, sending chills and thrills up the muscle boy's tree trunk-like leg.

"Ha, ha, ha, ha, ha, ha, ha, HOOOOo yeah, sure as shit Doc," Danny garbled, his massive upper body heaving under the binding strap stretched tight across it. "An-and with that damned lotion you and my dad smeared on my feet, ha, ha, ha, ha, ha, I-I'm even more ticklish now!! OOOOooooo ha, ha, ha, ha, ha, ha, ha!!!"

"Heh, when he was younger I used to tickle him like crazy Doc," Danny's father said, sliding his stick all over and around and around the bottom of his son's foot, holding it tight by the ankle in the restraint. "Every part of him was ticklish it seemed, his stomach area, his ribs, his armpits."

With his head thrown back Danny laughed louder and louder as the doctor held his foot tight with one hand, his fingers pressed against the bottom of it as he slid the stick-like device between the jock's toes.

"Please check between his toes on his other foot Mr. Smith," the doctor instructed the jock's father.

"Sure thing Doc," Danny's father replied.

"Har, har, har, har, har, har, ha, ha, ha, ha, ha, ha, ha!!!" Danny crowed. "OH JEEZ never knew that I was so ticklish between my toes Doc!!"

"Yeah, used to tickle the shit outa my boy here," Danny's father said the jock feeling even more humiliated as he recalled his dad tickling him when he was very young and feeling even more humiliated as his dad tickled him now. "But his feet were always the most sensitive. When his mom would have him wear thin nylon dress socks for family events, man that made him even more ticklish. Guess that nylon material against the skin makes it even more sensitive."

Danny's toes twitched involuntarily as the doctor and his dad worked the sticks in between them, rubbing the sensitive areas between the jock's toes. By now Danny was bathed in sweat as he was tickled more and more.

"Ha, ha, ha, ha, ha, ha, ha, ha!!!" Danny guffawed like crazy. "B-bet everyone in your waiting room can hear me Doc! Th-this is really embarrassin' let me tell you!!"

"Not at all young man," the doctor said. "All the examination rooms here in my lab are totally soundproof."

"Ha, ha, ha, ha, ha, ha!!!" Danny laughed the sound of his laughter mixing with the sound of the buzzing device in his hole, driving the muscle boy more than crazy at that point.

"I made sure to have the rooms made soundproof for the purposes of tests like this one," the doctor said and slid his stick up and down and up and down the bottom of Danny's foot.

"T-test?" *You call this a test?"* Danny said in between laughing and trying to catch his breath. Y-you and my dad are tickling the tar outa me here Doc!!"

As Danny laughed and laughed uncontrollably his hard cock twitched and danced between his muscular legs, his balls more than throbbing at that point. Pre cum and beads of piss formed at the tip of his wide sexy slit.

"Damn man, I-I'm goin' to lose my piss if you guys keep tickling me like this Doc," the jock pleaded beseechingly. "Ha, ha, ha, ha, ha, ha, ha, ha!!!"

"Oh no Danny, we can't have that now," the doctor admonished the well-muscled jock boy. "In a little while besides a blood test I'm going to need a urine sample from you."

"No pissing till the doc says so Danny boy," Danny's father said with total authority.

The doctor and his dad tickled the jock's feet more intensely, moving the sticks speedily between his twitching toes. Danny's feet twitched like crazy in the doctor's and his father's grasps and in the restraints. The lotion mixed with his feet sweat dripped to the floor, the scent seeming to be intoxicating.

"Th-then please stop ticklin' me Doc," Danny pleaded as his feet were tickled and tickled and tickled. "OOOOooooo ha, *ha, ha, ha, ha!!!"*

"It looks to me like the reflexes in your son's feet are working just fine Mr. Smith," the doctor said happily to Danny's father then turning his attention to the strapped down handsome young man. "It doesn't look like there will be a problem there when you get out on that football field."

"Gl-glad to hear it Doc," Danny chirped as the doctor and his father still went on rubbing the sticks over the bottoms, the arches and in between the toes of his big feet. "Ha, ha, ha, ha, ha!!!"

"I got to tell you Doc, I'm glad to hear it too, and even though we're drivin' my boy here crazy it does my heart good to hear him laughing like this," Danny's father said, seeming to be staring intently at his son's foot. "Means that his reflexes are in perfect order."

Finally, after what seemed like more than an eternal few minute's the doctor and Mr. Smith stopped tickling the jock's feet. Doctor Rack took the stick-like device from Danny's father and placed both of them in a jar of sterilizing liquid. Then, standing between Danny's spread legs he slowly slid the buzzing thermometer out of the jock's hole while Danny's father watched.

"UHHH GuuuuuuHHH, j-jeez," Danny gasped as the thing slowly came out, caressing the walls of his slicked hole with each second.

"Okay, it looks like the thermometer has done its work," the doctor said with satisfaction, pulling it the rest of the way out of the jock's slimy hole.

Danny was feeling beyond embarrassed and humiliated when he farted loud and smelly as the thermometer was taken from his hole.

"OHHHRRRRRR S-sorry Doc, sorry Dad, couldn't help that," Danny said with half a smile on his handsome face.

"Not to worry Danny, that's a perfectly normal reaction when a device of this size is extracted from your anus," the doctor said, not even commenting on how smelly the fart was. "Now, let's see what we have here shall we?"

"See that Doc?" Danny's father piped up and grabbed one of his son's nipples between his thumb and first two fingers. "Not only does my boy have nice meaty man tits like his old man here, but he also farts real nasty and macho like me too."

"D-dad, please," Danny gasped as his dad really squeezed and tugged his nipple.

The doctor held up the thermometer and smiled at the stretched out strapped down jock. If Danny's head weren't spinning and if his dad hadn't been tweaking one of his nipples he would have sworn that the doctor took a few hearty sniffs of the thermometer as he read it.

"Perfect Danny, no fever," Doctor Rack said happily. "So far you are getting a clean bill of health."

"I-I'm glad to hear that Doc," Danny whimpered as the doctor reached under the table and turned the lever.

Danny's muscular body was once again upright on the table.

"Got to tell you Doc, that stuff we smeared on my boy's feet smells just like the stuff we slicked his shit chute with before," Mr. Smith said, letting go of Danny's nipple and then eyeing his son's dangling restrained feet almost lustfully. "I know it's not the same stuff, but it sure does smell good enough to eat."

"Well Mr. Smith, like the other medication we used it is edible," Doctor Rack explained. "I like to use medicines that are edible just in case some it happens to spray off the patients area that it's being applied to and accidentally hits my or my nurse's lips."

"Yeah, I hear you Doc, good enough to eat huh?" Danny's father asked and Danny's eyes opened in shock as his father squatted between his dangling feet.

"D-dad, what're you doing?" the jock croaked in disbelief as his father gripped one of his ankles, pulled his foot forward as much as the restraint would allow and slurped his big toe into his mouth. "UHHH j-jeez, *Dad!!!*"

Danny's father seemed to be in total ecstasy with his eyes squeezed shut as he gently caressed the bottom of his son's beefy slimy foot and sucked his big toe at the same time.

"D-dad, st-stop it," Danny whimpered, his cock twitching and swinging back and forth big and hard between his legs, his balls churning.

"When he was a baby I used to do this to him all the time Doc," Mr. Smith said and quickly slurped Danny's toe back into his mouth.

"Yes, so I see," Doctor Rack said, grinning fiendishly at Danny, seeming to tell him that he knew a secret that only he and the jock's father shared.

"God, but this stuff tastes great Danny boy," Mr. Smith said, sounding like he was in total ecstasy.

He slid his tongue over the topmost part of Danny's foot, holding the bottom of his foot gently in hand as he lapped the peppermint tasting medication off it.

"OHHH f-fuck," Danny whispered, looking down in utter disbelief as his dad licked his foot.

"Heh, it's not every day that I lick my boy's feet Doc," Mr. Smith said and switched to Danny's other foot, lapping the peppermint tasting medication off that one next and stealing sucks on his toes.

"Dad, we need to talk," Danny said softly.

"Okay, it's time for my coffee break Danny," Doctor Rack said to the jock. "I'll be back soon. Mr. Smith, would you care to join me?"

"Sure Doc, that sounds good," Danny's father replied, letting go of his son's foot and standing up. "Maybe we'll smear some coffee on my boy's feet and lick that off next, what do you say?"

Danny looked at his father angrily.

"Just kidding Danny boy," Mr. Smith laughed and gave one of the jock's nipples a mean squeeze and twist.

"Ayyyyy GOD," Danny grunted and again felt quivers spiraling over him from the sensations of his squeezed nipple.

"In the meantime Danny I'll send my nurse in to get a blood test and a urine sample from you," Doctor Rack said as he and the muscle boy's dad headed for the door of the examination room. "You uh, didn't eat or drink anything other than water before you came here today right Danny?"

"N-no Doc, I didn't," Danny replied. "F-figured you would want to take blood and urine from me, and all that."

"Good boy," Doctor Rack said from the doorway.

Danny grimaced and gulped hard as the doctor and his dad left the room, closing the door behind them. When they were gone and the door was closed Danny farted again...

"Jeez, what a crazy examination this is," Danny whispered and wrinkled his nose at the smell of his own fart. *"And what the fuck is up with my dad licking my damned feet?"*

His cock, still rock hard and oozing pre cum twitched between his legs, begging for release, begging to shoot that pent-up load of jock boy juice.

"Sorry bud, but with my hands all tied up like this I can't help you," Danny said sadly to his cock. "Jeez, I must really be losing it here, *talking to my damned cock."*

A few minutes later the door to the examining room opened and the male nurse walked in, carrying a length of elastic, an empty syringe and a thin flexible clear tube.

"Hey there Jock guy," the nurse said as he closed the door behind him. "Ready for your blood test? Shit, it smells like someone's been farting in here."

"Yeah, s-sorry about that bud," Danny said, trying to act as nonchalant as possible, given his present position atop the table. "After the doc took that big ol' thermometer out of my shit chute I couldn't help farting a few times."

The nurse sprayed some air freshener then stepped over to Danny's table.

"Yeah, that thermometer will do it every time," the nurse mused with a grin on his face and stuck two fingers into Danny's still exposed hole.

"HuuuuuuHHH," Danny gasped at the sudden intrusion and the nurse quickly pulled his fingers out.

Danny farted loud and smelly, twice.

"See what I mean?" the nurse asked and again inserted two fingers into the jock's slimy rectum, deeper this time.

"UHHHnnnnnn!!!" Danny blubbered and farted again when the nurse took his fingers out. "Fuck man, leave my hole alone huh?"

The nurse smiled, sprayed the air freshener again and said, "Just trying to prove a point Mr. Smith."

"Well, you proved it, now just get on with the damned blood test," Danny said angrily. "God got me farting like a dude who ate too many spicy Buffalo wings."

"As you say Mr. Smith," the nurse replied and stepped next to Danny's right arm.

He wound the length of elastic tightly around the muscle boy's upper biceps a few times before pulling it tight.

"Ouch," Danny grunted and the nurse began tapping his arm, getting a vein to pop.

"Please make a fist and open and close it a few times," the nurse instructed Danny.

The jock did as he was told.

"So, what do you think of Doctor Rack so far?" the nurse asked Danny, trying to make some sort of conversation Danny supposed.

"H-he's pretty thorough," Danny responded as the nurse went on tapping his arm while he continued opening and closing his fist. "I mean, I've never had to be strapped down to a table for a medical exam before."

"Yes I know, most people are surprised by that when they come here for the first time," the nurse said and slid the needle of the syringe into Danny's vein. "There we go. You can leave your hand open now Mr. Smith."

Danny grimaced for a second at the sudden pinch and then the nurse attached the thin clear tube to the needle.

"Okay, this tube is the size of two vials," the nurse said as Danny's blood started seeping slowly into it. "It will take about half a minute or so to fill it."

"Heh, just don't leave me empty bud," Danny laughed, trying to feign relaxation.

"I'll be taking a urine sample afterwards," the nurse said and brazenly took Danny's hardness in his hand. "I hope you have to urinate substantially and I hope you won't have problems urinating with an erection. Some guys that have come here seem to."

As he spoke he gave Danny's cock a few playful tugs.

"H-hey, let go of my damned cock you pervert," Danny suddenly blurted. "Oh Good God, I-I could shoot my damned load of power spunk any second now!! Fuck, between you, the doc and even my dad tugging at my cock like it was a play toy I swear I could blow a load like crazy!!"

"You really think so?" the nurse asked with a sinister looking smile playing across his lips.

"Fuck yeah man, what with all that slop the doc and my dad greased up my shit chute with, jeez, Doc said it could act like an aphrodisiac of some sort," Danny garbled as the nurse handled his most private part.

"HMMM, no sense in making a mess then," the nurse mused and let go of the muscle boy's cock.

"OOOOOHHH…" Danny moaned as he felt his pent-up juices retreat into his nuts again.

A feeling of frustration seemed to wash over him. Could it be that he actually wanted this male nurse to jack him off? Could it be that at that point he wanted *anyone* to jack him off, up to and including *his dad?*

Danny leaned his head back for a moment or two, thought about his dad jacking him off, thought about his dad licking his feet and even thought about his dad licking his anal hole. At these thoughts his cock twitched and then he glanced at his arm as his blood filled the thin tube.

"H-hey man, I mean, Nurse, th-that tube is nearly filled," Danny grunted, purposely cutting off the thoughts he'd just been having.

"So it is," the nurse said and stepped over to Danny's arm.

The handsome jock watched as the nurse dismantled the blood test attachments from his muscular arm and then placed a Band-Aid on the small pinprick that the needle had left behind.

"I'll need a urine sample now Mr. Smith," the nurse said to the strapped down muscle boy and took two small Dixie cups from a dispenser over the sink in the examining room.

The nurse stood between the jock's legs and again took his hard member in hand. He pointed Danny's cock straight down so that his wide slit was aimed precisely at the cup. Danny gasped as the nurse held his cock tight.

"Okay, I want you to fill this cup and then hold it," the nurse said, gently stroking the jock's cock. "I'll then ask you to fill the second cup? Got it?"

"Yeah, g-got it," Danny murmured, watching intently as the nurse stroked the tip of his cock, rubbing the pad of his thumb just under his slit. "But like you said bud, it ain't easy to piss with a boner the size of the one I got going on here. J-jeez, never stayed so hard for so long, gotta tell you."

"Just concentrate," the nurse said with a sinister looking grin. "And let 'er rip."

The nurse helped Danny along by giving his hardness a few more tugs...

Danny concentrated and then pissed long, hard and yellow into the cup, filling it almost instantly with his sour smelling stream.

"Good boy," the nurse said. "Now hold it."

Danny stopped pissing, the feeling awful as he needed to relieve himself still much more. The nurse placed the filled cup on top of a medicine cabinet next to Danny's blood sample, the smell of Danny's piss filling the air. Danny watched as the nurse put a cover on the cup and then held the second cup under the jock's slit, taking his hard cock again in hand.

"UHHH!!!" Danny groaned as he was handled.

"Fill'er up please," the nurse said with a smile.

Danny concentrated and again pissed long, hard and yellow into the cup…

"Okay, stop again please," the nurse said when the cup was filled to the rim.

Danny followed the nurse's instructions, but still needed to piss some more…

"Say Nurse, you think you can get me one more cup, maybe two?" Danny asked as the nurse busied himself covering the second cup of the jock's urine.

"Well, Doctor Rack specifically asked for only two cups of urine," the nurse said with his back turned to Danny.

"B-but I still need to piss man," Danny said, sounding almost angry. "Now that you got me started the least you can do is help me finish."

The nurse held up the two cups of Danny's urine samples.

"HMMM, real yellow," the nurse said softly.

"So, what of it?" Danny asked.

"Means you're dehydrated," the nurse explained. "You're going to have to start drinking a lot more water Mr. Smith. Being a football player you should know that."

"Yeah, yeah, sure thing bud, as soon as I'm out of here I'll stop at the first grocery store I see and buy a big bottle of Poland Spring," Danny quipped, seeing beads of piss forming over his wide slit. "But please man; just get another cup or two for me. Fuck, but I still got to piss like a goddamned racehorse."

"Actually you won't need to buy any mineral water Mr. Smith," the nurse said. "I can properly hydrate you right now. It'll just add a half hour or so more to your examination but I'm sure Doctor Rack won't mind."

"Huh?" Danny asked, trying his best to hold in his flow of piss, watching as the nurse opened the small refrigerator and took out a sixty-four ounce bottle of what looked like cold water. "Wh-what are you planning on doing here?"

"As I said, I'm going to properly hydrate you," the nurse repeated, placing the bottle on a small table and rolling it next to the table that Danny was on.

The nurse used the lever under the table to splay the muscle boy's legs apart all over again, thus putting his sopped and sore hole on display again.

"C-c'mon man, *I got to piss here,*" Danny complained. "Get me a cup or two; never mind what you're doing right now."

"I'll tell Doctor Rack that I'm hydrating you for a half hour," the nurse said, seeming to ignore the jock's complaints and protests. "That way he can see other patients in the meantime."

Danny's eyes opened wide in terror as the nurse took a length of semi thick rubber hose from a cabinet drawer.

"Wh-what are you going to do to me man?" Danny whimpered the need to piss starting to feel overwhelming.

Without a word the nurse inserted one end of the rubber hose slowly into the muscle jock's waiting hole.

"OHHH!!! OHHHrrrrr j-jeez," Danny blurted, craning his head forward to watch as the nurse slid the hose as far in as possible.

"Just lay back and relax Mr. Smith," the nurse instructed the jock.

"*Th-this is unfuckingbelievable!!!*" Danny gasped, as the hose was inserted inch by inch into him.

"As I said Mr. Smith, try to relax," the nurse repeated himself, sounding rather stern at that point.

Danny felt as if his hole were actually sucking the hose into itself. The sounds of squishing coming from his anus were not music to his ears.

"N-not easy to relax when you got to piss and you suddenly have a hose wedged up in your shit chute bud," Danny gasped and lay his head back down.

Danny felt more of a sucking sensation in his hole as the hose was inserted still further. The nurse proceeded to attach the other end of the hose to the water bottle after he opened it.

"Okay, let's see if I can get a good suction on this thing now," the nurse said nonchalantly.

Danny watched with eyes agape as the nurse turned the bottle on its side and squeezed the hose a couple of times. Suddenly, the water was being sucked up out of the bottle, through the hose and into the jock's hole.

"H-holy God," Danny squeaked as he felt the first drops of cold water inside himself. "C-couldn't you have just given me a glass to drink from man?"

"It's more efficient this way Mr. Smith," the nurse explained. "This way I can hydrate you much faster. If we were to do it with you drinking from a glass it would take upwards of two hours. As I said, this way only takes a half hour or so."

Danny grimaced self-consciously as the nurse seemed to be drinking in the sight of his sweaty massive chest and his erect nipples.

"T-tell me somethin' bud, the suit guy that I saw leave here while I was in the waiting room, did he get an examination like the one I'm getting now?" Danny asked the nurse, trying to get his mind off what was happening at the moment.

"No, he just came in for some results from a blood test that Doctor Rack did on him a few days ago," the nurse replied. "Why do you ask?"

"Well, it's kind of silly but I was telling my dad how I know from a buddy of mine who's dad is a banker that all those suit type guys wear long dark socks, up to their knees," Danny said, grinning. As Danny spoke the nurse stepped next to him and took one of his nipples in his thumb and first finger.

"OHHH, and, *and* I was wondering if Doctor Rack had strapped him up to the table like I am right now," Danny went on breathlessly as the nurse twirled his nipple. "And I was joking with my dad how the suit guy probably left his socks on because they were so long that they took too long to take off."

"HMMM, now that you mention it that suit guy did leave his socks on while Doctor Rack had him strapped to the table," the nurse said with a grin and twirled and squeezed Danny's nipple harder.

Danny's cock danced and bobbed between his legs as the sounds of the water siphoning into him filled the room and the nurse played brazenly with his nipple.

"You like guys in long dark socks Danny?" the nurse asked the muscle boy.

"Uh, no, I mean, I'm not sure at this point bud," Danny replied, looking down as the nurse really twisted the tar out of his nipple at that point.

Danny wasn't thrilled that this faggot nurse had a muscle jock like him totally at his mercy only because he was all strapped down and restrained. Danny knew that if he wasn't strapped to that table he would have made short work of the man tit squeezing male nurse.

"I also recall that the gentleman was squeamish about taking a blood test so Doctor Rack asked that in addition to strapping him to the table that I blindfold him," the nurse said and produced a long black silk cloth after letting go of Danny's nipple. "Doctor Rack said that it was better if the gentleman didn't watch as his blood was extracted from him. Just as it's probably better if you don't watch as I hydrate you. You do seem more than a tad disturbed at the moment."

Danny's nipple that had been squeezed and twisted tingled like crazy as the nurse tied the black cloth over his eyes.

"Hey, second time I'm bein' blindfolded here bud," Danny complained. "What's the point of this?"

"As I said, Doctor Rack feels that it's better if sometimes the patients don't watch what's happening to them. Just relax Mr. Smith."

The nurse again squeezed and twisted Danny's nipple.

"Yeah, yeah, whatever, now how about leaving my man tits alone and letting me piss?" Danny asked sarcastically.

"I'll take care of that when I return in a half hour or so Mr. Smith," the nurse said, picking up the vials of Danny's blood and the cups containing his urine samples. "I need to get this stuff down to our lab technician."

"B-but," Danny pleaded the feeling of the water seeping into him already making him have to piss more.

"I'll tell Doctor Rack and your dad that you're being hydrated," the nurse said as he headed for the door to the room. "Don't worry; I'll take care of everything."

"T-tell my dad to come in here, *right away,*" Danny said as the nurse left the room, closing the door behind him. "OHHH JEEZ MAN…"

Danny squirmed miserably atop the table under the tight binding straps…

In what seemed like no time he was sweating more and more profusely as the water from the bottle drained…*into him*… His blindfold felt matted to his face…

The need to piss was excruciating ten minutes later and the muscled jock did more than his damnedest to keep his flow in check… Danny felt the walls of his hole literally sucking at the hose encased between them and the water flowed and flowed into him. He clenched his restrained hands into big meaty fists, leaned his head back and gasped and grunted.

Five more minutes past and then Danny's cock was harder than hard, oozing pre cum, oozing beads of piss and throbbing with a life all its own…

"OHHH…" he groaned miserably, his stomach starting to churn. "God, blindfolding me sure doesn't help stop the need to piss…*Fuck, that pervert nurse is givin' me an enema!!!*"

Twenty minutes into being hydrated Danny's head was more than spinning and he grimaced miserably behind the blindfold as he staunchly tried not to piss…

"Oh God Dad, why did you bring me here?" Danny whimpered and then heard the door to the examining room open.

He looked around dumbly with his blindfolded eyes.

"Wh-who's there?" the well-muscled jock called out. "Is that you Dad?"

"It's me Sir, your nurse," Danny heard the reply.

"Wh-where's my dad?" Danny asked as he heard the nurse come over to him.

"Out in the waiting room having coffee," the nurse replied as the sounds of the water seeping into Danny's rectum filled the room. "Looks like you're almost done here."

"Y-you didn't tell him to come in here like I asked you to man," Danny said angrily as the nurse sidled up next to the table.

"Okay, five more minutes and then I'll stop the flow," the nurse said and gave one of Danny's nipples a squeeze.

"Fuck, *fuck,* guy just loves my man tits," Danny groaned miserably. "Can you take the blindfold off me now?"

"I think it's better if we leave it on for now Mr. Smith," the nurse said, giving the knot in the back of the blindfold a tug. "Let's wait till we're done here."

"*Whatever,*" Danny said sarcastically. "But I got to tell you bud, I've never had to be blindfolded for any medical exam in the past."

"Still need to piss Mr. Smith?" the nurse asked the strapped down muscle jock.

"What do you think man?" Danny replied in question. "Shit, I feel like my insides are at the bursting point."

The nurse smiled and gave Danny's hard on a quick tug or two, getting a good loud gasp out of the football jock.

"Okay, just thought I should tell you that when the doc comes back he's going to take a hernia test on you," the nurse said.

"W-wonderful," Danny chirped.

Then, the nurse glanced up at the clock on the wall and smiled at Danny.

"Done," he announced and took the hose out of the water bottle first.

Danny felt the flow into his rectum cease. The muscle boy breathed a loud sigh of relief. Then, the nurse began slowly extracting the hose from Danny's hole.

"H-hope you got that air freshener nearby bud," Danny said almost breathlessly. "I get the feeling I'm goin' to fart real nasty and smelly here."

The nurse simply smiled and then the hose was out of Danny's hole. The jock felt a sudden draft as his hole was again on total display and true to his word he farted twice…

He and the nurse laughed…

"Oh God man, hurry up and get a few cups bud," Danny pleaded. "I'm goin' to piss now, no matter what!!"

"I think I'll need something a little bigger than a cup this time Mr. Smith," the nurse mused.

Danny heard the nurse rummaging around in the room and then felt a squishy device being slid over his erection.

"H-hey, wha-what're you doin' now Nurse?" Danny panted, his cock seeming to inflate as whatever it was, was slid tightly over it. "Come on man; take this blindfold off me already."

"Okay Mr. Smith, I suppose that's reasonable now," the nurse said. "Seeing as I'm just going to empty your bladder a little."

The nurse whisked the blindfold off the muscled jock leaving it dangling around his massive bull-like neck. Danny quickly looked down at his throbbing cock and saw that the nurse had encased it in some sort of latex sheath. The inside of the thing felt all squishy and slimy and smelled of peppermint. The muscle boy instantly guessed that the inside of the thing was greased up with the same stuff that the doc and his dad had used on his hole earlier. Attached to the sheath was a thin length of hose and the end of the hose was attached to a large beaker.

"H-holy shit man, y-you got my jock boy cock stuffed in that pump man," Danny gasped, still trying not to piss. "Wh-what's it goin' to do?"

"Nothing for the moment Mr. Smith," the nurse said. "Please urinate now if you would."

Danny leaned his head back, gasped loud, farted once and began pissing long, hard and white this time...

"There we go Mr. Smith, you're no longer dehydrated," the nurse said happily.

"HUUUUHHH j-jeez," the jock gasped, watching in disbelief as his stream filled the beaker slowly. "N-never had to piss so badly before."

Danny thrust his cock forward in the sheath as well as a guy who is strapped down could and it seemed like a river of floodgates opened up in him. He pissed more and more, his stream flowing easily through the hose and into the beaker.

"Fuuuuccckkk, th-that's some urine sample huh bud?" Danny asked the nurse with a grin.

"Sure is," the nurse replied and gave one of Danny's nipples a squeeze and twist, which for whatever the reason got the jock boy pissing even more.

"UHHH!!!" Danny gasped. "Fuck, seems like my man tits are the faucets for my pissing cock at the moment huh Nurse?"

"If you say so Mr. Smith," the nurse replied, watching as Danny's stream trickled freely into the beaker.

"W-was hydrating me so much really necessary bud?" the jock asked the nurse.

"I would think it was, seeing as your urine was a dark shade of yellow," the nurse said. "But look at it now."

"Y-yeah, nice and white," Danny said.

A few moments later Danny stopped pissing and marveled at the fact that the beaker was more than half-full.

"Jeez man, th-that had to be the longest piss I ever took," Danny said, practically breathlessly as the nurse took the end of the hose near his cock in hand.

"Hmmm, I gave you nearly sixty four ounces of water," the nurse said with a fiendish look in his eyes. "I can't believe you're done urinating already Mr. Smith."

The nurse gave the hose a tug and suddenly the sheath that Danny's cock was encased in came to sucking life.

"OHHH sh-shit man, holy crow and fuck it all bud," Danny grunted and bucked involuntarily under the binding straps. "Th-that thing is suckin' my cock!! I can feel it nibbling at the tip of my slit man!!"

"That should help you in urinating some more Mr. Smith," the nurse explained as the jock was more than bathed in sweat and glistening with it at that point. "After the way I hydrated you I'm sure you need to relieve yourself some more."

"OHHH, n-never pissed like this before though bud," Danny gasped and then found himself pissing again, his stream trickling through the hose and into the beaker. "OHHH jeez…"

The nurse seemed to smile with a sadistic look of satisfaction on his face as the jock boy pissed and pissed…

"HUUUHHH, f-feels like it's never goin' to stop," Danny panted.

"Oh it will, eventually," the nurse said and gave the hose another tug.

The sheath around Danny's cock sucked him harder and the jock pissed still more so…

"OHHH man, wh-what'd you do that for bud?" Danny chirped. "Fuck, my cock feels all bloated stuffed up in that damned pump!!"

"It'll be done soon Mr. Smith," the nurse said reassuringly and gently stroked Danny's sweat sopped hair.

"Wh-when's my dad comin' back?" Danny asked, almost whimpering.

"Soon Mr. Smith," the nurse replied. "He and Doctor Rack are almost done with their coffee break."

When Danny was finally, *finally* done pissing the beaker was just about filled to the rim with his piss.

"Oh man, fuck, that had to be the longest piss in human history," Danny said, sounding almost proud of himself.

"Yes, I would almost agree with you Mr. Smith," the nurse said, taking one end of the hose out of the beaker of the jock's piss.

The smell of Danny's white warm piss filled the air around them as the nurse then slowly took the latex sheath off Danny's cock.

"OHHH..." Danny groaned as the slimy sheath came off his hard cock, caressing his shaft at the same time.

"See? That wasn't all that bad now was it?" the nurse asked the muscle boy as he put a stopper in the beaker.

"W-well, when anything like that is over with and done it doesn't seem all that bad," Danny said softly, looking at the nurse, feeling exhausted by then.

"Okay, now before I go on to my next rounds Doctor Rack wanted one more thing from you," the nurse said, stepping over to a long cabinet and opening it.

"Wh-what was that?" Danny asked the nurse as the nurse took an odd looking machine out of the cabinet.

"A *few* sperm samples," the nurse said and Danny gulped loud, his face turning nearly pale white...

MY FIRST LIFT AND CARRY

Written by Mike, the Guy Lifter and
added onto by Christopher Trevor

I'm an average sized and average looking twenty-eight year old guy with an okay build. I've never worked out but I am abnormally strong at only five feet nine inches tall and one hundred and eighty pounds. My fetish is for getting into humiliating big, cocky, and full of attitude muscle boys and men. I get so sick of these guys strutting around the halls at school or at the mall who intimidate other guys. You know who they are, the tough guys and bullies who wear wife beater t-shirts, who go around showing off their muscles, strutting around like they are God's gift to women and thinking also that they are better than everyone else. I enjoy getting them into a spot so that they cannot decline a strength based challenge...and then completely humiliate them strength-wise in front of their friends until they are begging me to stop.

And I am sure like me; you know that the majority of cocky macho overly inflated ego men never EVER turn down a challenge. If they did it would be a blow to their machismo and manly pride.

I was at the beach the other day when this happened, what I want to share with you here. I ran into these two very well-built college hunks that were meanly picking on the younger/smaller brother of one of them. The kid was fifteen or sixteen years old and only about five feet six inches tall and maybe one hundred and thirty pounds…and the two big college dudes had to be at least twenty years old and around six feet tall with two hundred pounds of solid muscle on their frames. I was sitting near where I could keep my eye on the action that was unfolding and could not believe the shit that they were saying. I finally walked up to them and said, "Hey, why don't you leave the kid alone and go pick on someone your own size?" They turned, looked at me and told me to mind my own business… and to get lost. I said, "Not until you leave the kid alone." They both snickered and said that I was in no position to be demanding that and that if I didn't leave them alone they would put a world of hurt on me.

I took a couple of steps back, looked them over and said that they had most impressive builds and added that I wanted to know how much weight they could lift. Laughing, they began flexing and bragging about how very strong they were and then one of the dudes said, "I could lift you and my little brother at the same time."

"Oh really?" I replied. "So what, I only weigh about one hundred and seventy pounds, maybe one hundred and eighty and I would guess your little brother there to be about one hundred and thirty pounds…so that's only about three hundred pounds."

My reply seemed to make him mad and then he said, "Not many guys my age and size could do that."

I smiled from ear to ear in a mocking way and said, "Bet I could."

He then said, "NO WAY LITTLE MAN," and started laughing. I said, "I'll do you one better. I'll bet that I can lift you and your pal there at the same time and hold you both up off your feet *and* carry you around for at least five minutes. They looked at each other in amazement, laughed harder and said that there was no way that I could lift the two of them at once.

I asked if either of them thought they could military press the other above his head and they both said, "Sure, he's only two hundred pounds." I told them to prove it. Each tried, but neither could get the other up for reps and were somewhat surprised and angry that they couldn't do it. I then told them that I could military press them and of course they said, "No way." One of the guys stepped toward me and said, "Prove it," and in a fast motion I grabbed him and up he went. If you could have seen the look on his face as his feet suddenly left the sandy ground and the look on his friend's face as I stood there in the middle of the beach pressing this stud for reps. He was wailing about and saying stuff like, "Damn, you are a strong little dude," and "I can't believe you're doing this to me," and "This just ain't happening." As I cranked out my sixth or seventh rep with him I could feel him getting hard. I finally put him down after cranking out ten good reps with him and whipped down his gym shorts for all to see his throbbing hard-on. He was so embarrassed. I said, "It would seem that you are turned on by strength muscle boy." He became even more embarrassed and ran off.

I then grabbed the second dude and threw him up across my shoulders and started doing squats with him while he was yelling for the first dude to come back. I said that I wasn't finished showing off yet because I had not yet lifted the two of them together. Of course his younger brother was there cheering me on and other friends of theirs had gathered and could not believe what they were seeing.

These two guys were "THE GUYS" of their crowd/posse. Now they were being out-muscled, over-powered and manhandled by a much younger and much smaller dude. Of course I loved it and had a raging hard-on myself. Once I cranked out twenty-five or so squats with the dude, he was begging me to put him down… I told him I wouldn't put him down until he jacked me off. He said he wasn't into that stuff and I said that he wasn't going to have a choice in the matter. He would have to jack or suck me off or get his friend out there to do it before I would even consider putting him down. He started screaming for his friend to come out and save him. I started carrying him up toward the private beach house where his mouthy and full of attitude friend had run into. His other friends started to follow and I told them to stay back as I carried the dude up the stairs out onto the deck and stood there for all his friends to see me, this little dude manhandling their big college jock friend.

"C'mon man, put me down already, huh?" he pleaded and I simply grinned meanly.

His friend finally came out and I put the dude down. I then instructed them to stand side by side. They did as I had told them; I walked up to them, bent down, put my head in between them and told them both to lie across my shoulders. Again they did as I had told them. I stooped up, lifting both of them at the same time (one over each shoulder.) I then walked over to the rail of the deck holding the two of them up across my shoulders in a fireman carry for all below to see. Their friends could not believe what they were seeing. They were cheering me on and I was feeling really good. I carried the two dudes down the stairs and out onto the beach. I finally put them down but some girl in the crowd yelled, "Lift them up in your arms…carry them around like the little girls that they are." I grabbed one of the dudes, picked him up into my arms (cradle style) and strutted around, jostling him a bit as I did. Some guy said, "See if you got the power to lift/hold/carry them both like that at the same time." The guys said, "Hell no…he cannot lift us both in a cradle, it's impossible." Well of course that encouraged me so I tried it…and shit…I even surprised myself. I had a raging hard-on.

I carried them back up the stairs onto the deck and put them down. I asked them which one wanted to be curled. Neither guy said that I could of course…but I did… I cranked out ten good curls with the guy. I noticed that while I was curling him, his big dick got hard up against my bicep. I put him down and said that it was time that the two of them showed me some respect for what I had just done. I lifted one of them up across my shoulders in a fireman carry and instructed the other to suck me off. The dude was hesitant, but then he said, "Man you earned it. You're the strongest guy of any age/size I've ever met. It's fucking amazing how strong you are. I'll suck you off."

I will never forget that night.

CAPTAIN HEALEY TAKES HIS CP

Written by Christopher Trevor

SWISH-CRACK SWISH-CRACK SWISH-CRACK-SWISH-CRACK-SWISH-CRACK-SWISH-CRACK-SWISH-CRACK were the sounds that were emanating from behind the closed door of the major's private office conference room, Major Anthony Nelson to be exact. And in between the sounds of the willow-switch swishing through the air followed by the sound of that switch connecting to bared ass flesh as it came down fast and hard, were the sounds of a soldier, a handsome, robust, muscular and well-toned soldier, Captain Roger Healey, he screaming and hawing in a man's true pain.

"ARRRRRRRRRRR!!! PLEASE SIR MAJOR NELSON!" Captain Healey, an outstanding and exemplary soldier, exemplary until that moment it seemed, cried out loud yet pitifully as the thin willow-switch connected over and over and over with his bared ass flesh…as he lay across the large conference table in his commanding officer's office conference room, tied at the wrists to the table, his arms spread out and wide and the slack of the rope tied off to the table legs under the structure he lay on.

SWISH-CRACK   SWISH-CRACK   SWISH-CRACK-SWISH-CRACK-SWISH-CRACK-SWISH-CRACK-SWISH-CRACK went the major's willow-switch, him stripped of the upper portion of his immaculate uniform to a beige colored tee shirt, wearing his olive colored uniform trousers and spit-shined black lace-up army issued dress shoes as he did his work, his muscular arm raised and then coming down hard as he beat the naked ass of his underling, over and over, relentlessly with the accursed willow-switch.

The major was sweating as he did his work, what he felt was not just his work, but his duty, his responsibility as an officer to punish and to show his wayward underling the error of his ways… and through reddening and welting the captain's bare buttocks he would do just that…

"PLEASE SIR, PLEASE MAJOR NELSON, NO MORE, OH GOD SIR, NO MORE!!!" Captain Healey pleaded in a high crescendo sounding voice as the major stood over him, breathing heavily in between raps and swats on the captain's ass cheeks…with his willow-switch.

"Captain, we are just getting started here," the major intoned, sounding every bit the army man, the army soldier that he was, holding the willow-switch tight in his grip with one hand and caressing the red, red, ass of his underling with the other. "I plan to make this rump of yours, and other parts of you so hot and red that the men will be able to fry eggs on it for their breakfast come the morning…"

"OH GOD, OH PLEASE SIR, I-I don't think I can take much more of this..." the tied down, stripped to his black cotton knee socks wailed. "And I seriously doubt Sir that the men would want to eat eggs for breakfast that were fried on my naked ass cheeks!"

The major smiled sadistically, rubbed the captain's red ass cheeks with his willow-switch and said, "Spread those sexy gams for me Captain, and be quick about it."

With his eyes filled with tears and more tears streaming down the cheeks of his boyishly handsome face the captain did as he had been ordered. He spread his legs wide, exposing his low-hanging dangling testicles in their hairy sac and his shriveled cock as it lay over his testicles. He involuntarily hoisted himself to his gold toed toes...thus spreading his legs wider yet...exposing the pink of his bunghole for his commanding officer. The sense of humiliation that the captain felt at that moment was like none other he had ever felt before.

Captain Healey heard the sound of the major as he took a deep breath... and then the dreaded sound of the willow-switch as it swished high and in the air...

"RRRRRRRRRRRR OHHH NO!!!" the captain wailed, even before the willow-switch once again connected with his reddening ass cheeks.

CRAAAAACCCKKK

"So tell me Captain, will you ever again do to the men under your command what I caught you doing tonight?" the major asked loudly and brought his willow-switch down nearly ten times in hard succession on the rear-end of the captain.

SWISH-CRACK   SWISH-CRACK   SWISH-CRACK-SWISH-CRACK-SWISH-CRACK SWISH-CRACK SWICH-CRACK SWISH-CRACK SWISH-CRACK SWISH-CRACK

"AAAAAAHHHAAARRRRR NO, NO MAJOR NELSON SIR, NEVER, NEVER AGAIN SIR!" Captain Healey cried out, nearly roaring as he danced on his gold toed toes and his balls swung and twitched between his spread legs.

Then, to Captain Healey's utter dismay and further humiliation, the major reached down and between the captains' spread legs and helped himself to a handful of those dangling testicles…and squeezed them hard and unforgivingly.

"OWWW, OH GOD, please Sir, easy with my family jewels…" the captain pleaded.

The major held the captain's most private parts tight in his hand, pulled them forward and under the man's spread ass crack, and as he held Captain Healey's pride and joy in hand he again swatted and rapped the tied down man's ass cheeks with the dreaded willow-stick.

CRACK, CRACK, CRAAAACK, CRAAAACK, CRACCCK, was the sound as the switch connected again and again with the now seared flesh of Captain Healey's ass cheeks.

And as the major beat and swatted the captain's ass cheeks he meanly squeezed and pressurized his charge's balls in his hand…

"Tell me, tell me what it is you'll never do again Healey, tell me loud and clear, just so we're on the same page as to the reason of why I'm beating your ass to a red pulp here," Major Nelson commanded. "Tell me why I'm sweating here while I work so hard to show you the error of your ways, Captain."

"I-I'll never make my men suck my cock again Major Nelson Sir!" the captain screamed and in response the major brought his willow-switch down hard and fast again and again and again on the ass cheeks of Captain Healey.

With each swish, with each lash the captain felt a line of fire erupt across his naked buttocks…

The major was a stickler for the rules of the army. He didn't give a shit about "Don't Ask, Don't Tell" and he could have cared less if it had recently been repealed. When he had happened upon the captain having his pud sucked in his office by not one, but two of the privates under his command the major was beyond appalled and livid at the scene in front of him. There was Captain Healey, standing nearly at attention behind his desk with his manhood, his thick and long cock and kiwi sized balls sticking out of the fly opening of his uniform trousers…and there were two of the young privates under his command on their knees, licking the captain's balls and taking turns sucking his cock…it was reprehensible, it was unthinkable…it was an abomination in the standards and values that the army stood for…

When the major had happened to walk into the captain's office, only because he needed some papers signed by his underling and saw the scene in front of him he had nearly blanched…but being the professional and well-trained officer that he was, had been for the last fifteen years in fact, he quickly took stock and then charge of the situation. He had slammed the captain's door closed and locked it from the inside, the one thing that the captain, in his sexual frenzy had obviously forgotten to do when he had ordered the two privates to get busy servicing him. At the sound of the office door being slammed shut and locked the two privates had instantly stopped what they were doing and looked up from where they were kneeling.

"What in all fucks is going on here???" Major Nelson barked.

Looks of horror and guilt instantly spread over the faces of the three men, the two privates stayed rooted to the spot where they had been kneeling on the floor as they serviced their captain, and

Captain Healey stood suddenly totally at attention, mortified beyond reasoning with his erect cock sticking out of his uniform trousers along with his big saliva soaked balls.

"Uh, Major Nelson Sir, I-uh-I can explain…I think…" Captain Healey blurted and as he babbled stupidly one of the privates gripped one of his well-shined black shoed feet.

The captain took a hearty and deep breath…and felt his cum churning in his balls…because even though he loved having men under his command suck his cock, lick his balls, eat his asshole and even fuck him from time to time…it was when his goddamned size twelve hooves were toyed with that made him lose his load as he called it. And he knew that from where the two privates were kneeling that the major could not see that one of them had meanly and brazenly squeezed one of his shoed feet…intent on totally embarrassing the captain more than he already was it seemed.

"*Oh no…*" Captain Healey whispered and when the private let go of his foot he found himself shooting a whopper-sized load of soldier cum, all over his uniform jacket and necktie, and his cock wasn't even being touched or sucked at the moment.

"WHAT THE FUCKING FUCK HEALEY???" the major roared as he watched the man he commanded spew his load, thick ropes of jism erupting from the captain's piss hole over and over and over again.

"AAAAAHHH fuck, oHHH yeah," Captain Healey panted as he stood at attention shooting his load and his commanding officer looked at him in disgust and revulsion.

The two privates, still on their knees grinned at each other in a conspiracy-like manner…

When the captain was done shooting his load his uniform jacket and tie were smeared and coated with his sexy mess.

"HEALEY, what is this all about???" Major Nelson roared as he slowly approached the breathless captain, not believing what he was seeing as the thick white creamy fluid sluiced down his underling's uniform jacket and congealed on his necktie.

"It uh, it's not what you think Major Nelson Sir..." the captain began.

"SILENCE HEALEY! It is what I think! Do not try to make it otherwise! It is obviously and exactly what I think!" Major Nelson barked and then looked down at the two privates.

"You two, on your feet, NOW!!!" the major commanded.

As the two privates slowly got to their feet Captain Healey reached for his private parts to pack them up and back into his uniform trousers.

"HEALEY, STOP!!!" Major Nelson ordered.

"B-but Sir..." Captain Healey pleaded.

"You like being on display like that???" the major shouted as the two privates stood up and stood next to their captain on either side of him. "Then that's how you'll stay till I say otherwise!"

"Y-yes Sir!!!" Captain Healey responded feeling mortified with his family jewels on display, his cock dribbling out the last remnants of his juices, and his jism trickling down his uniform jacket and necktie.

The man could not believe how much sperm he had shot, and just from having one of his damned feet squeezed at that...

"You two!!" Major Nelson shouted at the two privates. "Clean the captain's mess off his uniform jacket and tie and then be on your ways. Healey, I'm going to deal with you in ways your sex-filled pinhead just can't imagine..."

The captain's eyes opened wide in horror, because he had heard the stories, the urban legends actually, of how Major Nelson dealt with his underlings who fucked up…and this was a truly major fuck up, Captain Healey knew…

The two privates shouted "Yes Sir!" in response to Major Nelson's order and then leaned down over their captain and got busy cleaning the cum off his uniform jacket and tie, with their tongues…

As one of the privates licked and slurped the captain's cum off his uniform jacket the other private quickly pulled the captain's cum stained tie out from his uniform jacket and began eating the mess of cum off it…

Major Nelson watched in awe as the two privates ate their captain's mess, it was obvious to him that the two men had not been forced or coerced into servicing their commanding officer. No, this was a mutual sex romp…but being the man he was and being the soldier he was and had been for the last fifteen years there was no way Major Nelson was going to tolerate this subversive behavior on his watch…

He allowed the two privates to take their time cleaning the captain's uniform jacket and his necktie. It was also not lost on the major how the captain was breathless…and again fully erect and at full-mast in the cock as he was so lovingly cleaned of his sexy eruption.

"Clean the captain's cock as well, I see him dribbling his mess there," Major Nelson called out as he watched the two privates doing their work.

It was the private who had squeezed Captain Healey's shoed foot earlier that was quickly on his knees and licking and lapping at the tip of his root, scoffing down the pre-seed that seemed to accumulate there over and over.

"No, no, don't…" Captain Healey whispered, as he felt the private's fingers diddling over one his army-issued shoes. "Please don't…it'll happen again Soldier, you know how horned I get when my feet are played with and…"

The private snickered meanly and gave the captain's foot a few hard squeezes…

Suddenly, like a damn opening the captain was gushing his load all over again…this time spewing his mess all over his uniform jacket, his shirt, his tie…and over the uniform of the private who had been still licking the captain's mess off his uniform jacket…

"OH GAWWWD, you bastard, you tricked me again," Captain Healy shouted down at the private as he breathlessly stood at attention and shot thick ropes of his mess all over again.

"Healey, silence!!!" Major Nelson ordered loudly. "Privates, out of here now, I'll take charge of the captain at this point!!"

"YES SIR!!" the two privates replied, saluted the major and quickly made their way out of Captain Healey's office, Major Nelson quickly locking the door again behind them.

When he turned back to the spewing captain a look of repugnance came over the major's face…

"What in all fucks is wrong with you Healey?" the major shouted. "Since when do you let men under your command suck you off and lick your balls???"

"I-I'm sorry Sir, I really am so sorry," the captain gasped, but still another rope of his jazz erupted from his cock. "OHHH JEEZ…"

"You make me sick Healey," the major said, stepping over to where the captain was standing, panting and gasping. "I know that when we started out here in the army we were the best of buds as two buddies could possibly be, BUT, I never expected something like this man!"

"S-Sorry Sir…" the captain replied as the major gripped his upper arm tight.

"The way I see it Healey you've got two choices here," Major Nelson seethed as he held tight to his underling's arm, his lips pressed nearly right into the captain's ear as he spoke.

"T-two choices Sir?" Captain Healy stuttered.

"Yes, you can either take the corporal punishment that I'll deal out to you personally in my office conference room…" Major Nelson said into the captain's ear, his lips grazing Healey's earlobe as he spoke. "Or tomorrow morning we can both report to the general's office where I'll report what I stumbled upon and you'll be court-martialed…along with your two boy toy's as well. What's your choice Healey???"

As his commanding officer gripped his arm the captain turned to look sideways at Major Nelson.

"What time should I be in your office conference room Sir?" Captain Healey asked.

The major smiled, let go of the captain's arm and looked at his watch.

"It's ten after five now,' Major Nelson said. "I'll come back here for you at six sharp. Everyone will have left the base for home by then. It'll just be the two of us here. It's going to be my pleasure to bring you to my office conference room personally…"

"Personally Sir?" Captain Healey asked, wondering why he needed his commanding officer as an escort.

"Just be ready Healey, in the interim I'll prepare for your CP," the major said.

"Y-yes Sir Major Nelson," Captain Healey replied as his CO headed for the door to his office.

After the major slammed out of Captain Healey's office he breathed a loud sigh of relief...

"Okay, no court martial for me, no court martial for my two sex slaves, but fuck, corporal punishment???" Captain Healey whispered.

He looked down at his exposed cock, his dangling balls and his uniform jacket, shirt and tie all smeared with his man juices...

At six PM Major Nelson returned to Captain Healey's office and entered without knocking...

At ten after six PM Captain Healey's officer door opened again and Major Nelson exited, with his underling in tow. Holding the captain by his upper arm with one hand and his fingers of his other hand twined in the captain's wavy brown hair Major Nelson led the mortified stripped to his knee length black cotton socks and blindfolded with his cum soaked tie captain down the corridor.

"Oh God, Major Nelson Sir, please, this is humiliating," Captain Healey pleaded, his hands placed strategically over his shriveled cock between his legs as he was led along in total darkness. "This is not CP Sir, this is degrading!"

"No more humiliating than being caught with your cock in a private's mouth or shooting your load in front of your commanding officer all over your uniform," Major Nelson seethed and twined his fingers harder in the captain's hair. "What was humiliating and degrading was seeing that uniform of yours soaked with your cum... no way was I going to allow you to wear that uniform to my office conference room..."

"Oh please Sir, what am I in for?" the captain asked, wondering why in all fucks besides having been ordered to strip to his socks he was also blindfolded.

"You'll find out soon enough Captain," the major replied and then led the befuddled captain into his spacious office conference room.

Captain Healey heard the door to Major Nelson's office conference room slam shut and then Major Nelson whipped the blindfold off his charge…

With his hands still placed over his crotch area the captain saw the willow-switch and other implements spread out on the major's desk.

"Oh holy shit," Captain Healey whispered and stood rooted to the spot in his tall black socks as he watched the major taking off his uniform jacket, his tie and then his shirt, stripping his upper muscular body down to his beige colored army tee.

"Like I said Healey, it's either this…" Major Nelson said as he hung his jacket, shirt and tie on a coat rack. "Or we can meet tomorrow morning in the general's office for a formal court-martial."

As Major Healey took a deep breath Major Nelson held up the captain's cum soaked necktie.

"And I will bring the evidence along for the court-martial Healey," Major Nelson said, almost mockingly.

"No Sir, please, not that, I agreed to corporal punishment and corporal punishment I will accept," the captain pleaded. "I enjoy being in the army and don't want to be court-martialed Sir!"

The major smiled sadistically, stepped over to his desk, opened a bottom drawer, and brought out a goodly amount of white cotton rope.

"Okay Healey, spread yourself out across the conference table dead-center," Major Nelson ordered. "And stretch your arms out as far as possible…"

As Captain Healey did as he was told he realized that with the position he would be in his well-rounded ass cheeks would be on full display...his cock and balls would dangle freely below his ass crack...his inner thighs and lower legs would be easy targets...all for the major and his willow-switch...and for the other ass reddening implements that the major had laid out.

When Major Nelson turned around from his desk he saw that his charge was laying splayed dead-center across the oak conference table with his muscular arms splayed long and wide...

The two men had been friends for a long time since they had joined the army together, fifteen years ago. Anthony Nelson had come from California to sign up and Roger Healey was a native New Yorker. When they met the two men were instant buddies. It was not lost on either of them that their names, Anthony Nelson and Roger Healey were the names of two famous fictional military buddies from the long ago TV show "I Dream Of Jeannie" and that they were just as handsome in their uniforms as the two actors who had portrayed those military men were. But it was Anthony Nelson who had risen to the rank of "Major" and Roger Healey had only made it as far as "Captain", and even though they were good buddies Anthony Nelson never once let his friend know who was now the CO, the commanding officer, the head honcho, the big cheese so to speak...

As he squatted down to lash the captain's wrists to the table by winding mounds of rope around his wrists and securing them to the table legs under the oak structure the major's own cock swelled in his uniform pants. Whenever he had to subject an underling to CP it always boned him up real hard it seemed...

Once the captain was secured to the table and looking like a sacrificial sort of victim splayed out on an altar the major picked up his willow-switch...

"I would usually do this in rounds of thirty swats at a time Healey, but that would be for normal military offenses," the major said as the captain looked up at his superior officer in dread.

And that was when the swishing of the willow-switch through the air had begun, and for each flight it took through the air it landed hard and unforgivingly on the captain's upturned ass cheeks...

CRACCCK CRACCCKKK CRACCCKKK CRACCCKKK CRACCCKKK

"HOOOOO, HOOOOOO, OH PLEASE STOP MAJOR NELSON!!!" Captain Healey blubbered, and the major's thoughts returned to the present.

The major had not been keeping a count of how many swats he had administered to his charge's rear end, but it looked like the captain had accidentally sat down on a hot waffle iron, his ass cheeks were that seared at that point...

The major decided at that moment that his underling had had enough thrashing with the willow-switch. It was time to change gears...and implements...

As the thrashing ended the silence in the major's office conference room was nearly deafening, broken only by the captain's loud and profuse crying...his poor ass felt like it was in flames... and he knew from the implements laid out on the major's desk that there was still more to come.

The captain squirmed miserably atop the conference table and watched in horror as the major next picked up a thin wooden cane...

"OH GOD, no wonder you tied me down for this Major," the captain cried.

Major Nelson stepped to the table to look over his handiwork, namely how well he had reddened and primed his buddies ass cheeks for the more intense handiwork that was soon to come...

He placed a large hand on one of the captain's pulsing cheeks and then allowed that hand to move casually over Captain Healey's lower rump and thighs. As he caressed the captain's thighs Major Nelson took in the sight of the captain's well-shaped socked feet as he stood on his tip toes, his gold toe tip toes that was...

"Plant your feet flat on the floor Healey," the major ordered then.

Shaking like a leaf Captain Healey did as he was told and Major Nelson raised the cane...

"OH NOOOOO, NOOOO!!!" the captain shrieked, even before the wood connected with his already wounded buttocks.

WHACCCKKK WHACCCKKK WHACCCKKK WHACCCKCKKK were the sounds of stinging as the cane flew through the air and landed on the captain's red ass cheeks, now those cheeks being dutifully striped...

Captain Healey's shrieks of pain were now mixed with screams of torment; it was actually one constant howl of fury as he was caned rapidly and in awful succession...

"AAAAHHHYOWWWEEEE!!!" the captain screamed, sounding like a female opera singer at the feeling of the unbelievable burning in his poor butt.

As he was now caned, as his ass cheeks were being quickly striped Captain Healey bounced around on the tabletop like a mad puppet of sorts, and Major Nelson was the puppeteer... But he could do nothing to escape the barrage of thrashes from the cane as the ropes about his wrists secured him tight and held him to the table. His mouth was open now in a constant "O" of outrage as he was madly caned... The poor captain Healey howled the sonic equivalent of his rear end's pain...

As his superior officer now caned his behind he could feel the stripes happening...and the welts that would eventually bubble to the surface. Captain Healey wondered just how much one soldier's ass cheeks could take.

After what felt like what had to be more than sixty swats from the cane Captain Healey was a blubbering, sweating, screaming and pain-filled mess as he lay atop the table, tied down tight and squirming...

"PLEEEEAAASE MAJOR, please, I beg of you, NO MORE!!!" Captain Healey squealed madly, feeling almost insane with the pain that was his rupturing rump.

"Sorry Roger, but this is for your own good," the major replied and raised the cane high.

"NOOOOOO, NOOOOOO!!! This is beyond CP now Sir!" Captain Healey thundered and screamed in massive pain anew as the cane this time connected with the backs of his beefy thighs. "YOWWW!!!"

The major swatted and swiped the captain's inner thighs nearly twenty times with the cane before resuming the caning of his now crimson, striped ass cheeks...

"AAAYAYYYYEEE!!!" Captain Healey wailed his head up off the table and facing forward as a waterfall of tears streamed from his eyes and down his cheeks.

The major then alternated caning the captain's ass cheeks and his inner thighs...swatting and swiping crazily, lifting the cane higher with each blow...

The pain in Captain Healey's ass cheeks at that point felt like a pan of boiling water had been tossed over it, and his inner thighs weren't faring so well either by then.

"AAAAAHHHRRRRRRRRHHH!!!" the captain roared in pain, bile flowing from his wide open mouth and onto the table he was lashed to at the wrists.

When Major Nelson finally put the cane down on his desk Captain Healey's ass and inner thighs were striped, welted and pulsing with heat...

The beaten man lay on the table gasping for air, breathing unevenly at that point, snot dripping from his nose and onto the table along with his bile...

"Tell me Healey, tell me what I want to hear," the major said. "Tell me what you'll never do again!"

"I'm so sorry Major Nelson Sir, I am sOOOO sorry," Captain Healey shrilled. "I will never, ever again have the men under my command suck my cock...or service my nipples...or lick my balls... or fuck my ass...NEVER AGAIN SIR!!"

"Fuck Healey, you mean to say that you let the men in your command fuck you in the ass?" the major asked and the captain instantly regretted his confession.

"I-I-Sir, as I said, it will never happen again...SIR!!!" the captain thundered and begged as he watched his CO pick up two more lengths of rope. "OH GOD SIR, what now??? Please, I've learned my lesson, I really have!!! OH GOD NO!!!"

Then, the captain was laying atop the table, feeling terror stricken as the major squatted behind him and began winding rope around and around each of his black socked ankles...and then spreading the captain's legs as far apart as possible and tying the slack of the rope around his ankles to the table legs...

Captain Healey felt as if he were the main course at a sadistic themed Thanksgiving dinner, feeling like the spread out turkey in the center of the table.

"Please Major Nelson, no more, PLEASE..." Captain Healey continued to beg.

As the major was squatting at one of the captain's now tied socked feet he trailed his fingertips over the captain's calves, just above where his tall socks ended...

Without a word Major Nelson got to his feet and stepped over to his desk...

This time he picked up a length of rubber hose...

"Bad enough you have the men under your command suck your cock, bad enough you have them nurse on your tits like you were a woman or something like that, bad enough you let them lick your balls Healey," the major said as he approached with the length of rubber hose. "But to let them fuck your hole, now that is just unacceptable Captain!"

That said, the major took up position next to Captain Healey's left bound leg and raised the rubber hose high.

"Besides having trouble sitting tomorrow Healey, you're also going to have trouble walking," Major Nelson stated harshly and brought the rubber hose down hard on the back of Captain Healey's calf, right above his tall sock.

SWATTTTTT

"OOOOHHHRRRRR..." Captain Healey roared anew. "OH GOD NO, not my calves too Sir, please, not my calves too!!!"

The major swung the rubber hose again and again and again, connecting harder and harder with Captain Healey's right calf.

"YOWWW!!!" the captain reeled crazily, the stinging pain from his calf seeming to slither down into his socked foot.

"Captain Healey, know this and know it now, and KNOW IT WELL," Major Nelson thundered as he then shifted on his feet, raised his rubber hose and aimed it at the open crack of the tied down captain's asshole.

"When SELF-Discipline is lacking in a man in uniform, then DISCIPLINE must AND WILL BE imposed!"

Then, to the captain's horror the major whacked and wracked his exposed asshole with the length of rubber hose...

After a while the captain had no more voice left to scream with...he was a totally beaten man...

By the time the major was done rubber hosing his hole, Captain Healey's ass was a crimson mess of red stripes and welts, his inner thighs were red and pulsing, his calves just above his black socks were as shiny red as a fire engine and his asshole felt as if it had been ruptured. He dreaded when the need to take a dump would come...

"All I can say Roger is that I hope you're learning your lesson here tonight," the major said as he stepped in front of the captain's face.

Captain Healey looked up and was about to say that he was indeed learning his lesson, and then some, but was instantly speechless when he saw the major standing there with his cock sticking out of the fly opening of his uniform trousers, along with a pair of the biggest sweatiest and pulsing balls the captain had ever seen.

"UH, Sir?" Captain Healey began but then his words were cut short as the major slid his semi hard cock into his mouth.

As the major's cock passed over his trembling tear-soaked lips the captain found himself slurping hard to get as much of the cock into his mouth as possible, as quickly as possible.

"AH yeah, there you go Healey," Major Nelson grunted heartily. "Suck your major's cock buddy, just want to give you a taste and feel of what the men under your command have been getting from you."

As Captain Healey sucked the major's cock it grew hard in his mouth and he tasted the sweat of the day and the remnants of piss on his commanding officer's manhood. Major Nelson cupped the captain's chin in his hand and Captain Healey looked up and into the eyes of the man who had just performed the most intense form of CP he could remember receiving in a long time...

As the captain sucked cock his red ass, inner thighs, calves and beaten asshole tingled and pulsed with lives all their own it seemed. Underneath him the captain's cock tingled long, hard and beefy...

The major moaned and groaned in sexual abandon as he held the captain's cupped chin in his hand, forcing him to look up and into his eyes as he slid his cock in and out of the man's mouth.

"OH YEAH, getting close here Healey," the major grunted. "Tell me, do you make your underlings swallow your soldier jism when they suck your cock?"

With his mouth filled with cock the captain nodded "Yes."

"Then you too shall swallow jism, your major's jism," Major Nelson said with a mean looking grin.

He then increased his pace as he slid his cock in and out of his charge's craw, his big sweaty balls slamming against the bottom of Captain Healey's chin as he fed and fed him.

"RRRRMMMFFFF..." Captain Healey swooned as he felt his own balls churning beneath him.

"OH yeah, and after you swallow this blast of my jism I'm gonna punish you some more Healey," the major said, swooning now, gripping the captain's chin tighter in his hand and caressing the back of the captain's neck with his other hand. "I have a thin-handled hairbrush over there with your name on it bud..."

As he continued to suck the major's cock new tears formed in the captain's eyes...

He had seen the thin-handled wooden hairbrush alongside the other spanking implements that the major had used on him, but didn't think it would be used on him at that point. As Captain Healey went on sucking cock he cried miserably.

"Now, now Healey, you should have known that your CP was far from done at this point," the major chuckled as he jammed his cock deep in his charge's throat. "Did you think that just because you sucked my cock that we were done? No way Healey, no fucking way! OH YEAH, there you go buddy, deep throat your major's meat stick for him...feels great..."

With Major Nelson's cock deep down in his throat the captain found it difficult to breathe, he choked a few times and his eyes rolled in his head, and then the major slowly slid his erection back up and into the Captain Healey's velvety feeling mouth.

As he sucked and suckled his CO's cock Captain Healey realized how in the fifteen years that he and Major Nelson had known each other the two men had never seen each other's private parts. Even when they had gone through basic training together they never changed out of their gear together. As he sucked the major's cock harder yet the captain realized how it took this particular event to bring the two men together in such a twisted yet somehow sensuous fashion.

"OH MAN, getting there Healey, gonna feed you a nice nutritious snack here," the major panted. "And then after I punish you hairbrush-wise I'll fuck that reddened hole of yours for you..."

"RRRRRMMMFFFFFF!!!" Captain Healey protested around the major's cock in his mouth.

"Oh, what?" the major asked. "You think you're too good and too much of a man and too much of a soldier to take it up the ass Healey? I REALLY want you to know how your underlings felt bud…and taking my second erection up your hole will really make you know how they felt."

The captain nodded "NO" over and over again around the major's cock in his mouth, but his pleadings went unheard, and then he tasted what was the major's crème de la crème as his superior officer began spurting his load…

"OH FUCK me man, fuck me, OHHH, feels great to be feeding you my load Healey," the major swooned, dancing sort of sexily and stupidly as he shot his load and shot his load.

When the major was done he let his cock slip slowly from Captain Healey's mouth.

"Better not have lost a drop of my precious pearly juices Healey," the major warned as he grabbed the captain by a handful of his wavy hair and slammed his balls against his trembling lips. "Lick my nuts bud."

With no choice in the matter it seemed Captain Healey stuck out his cum coated tongue and bathed the major's testicles with it.

"OHHH FUCK YEAH, fuck me hard man, but that's awesome, just love having my nuts licked after I shoot a load, nothin' else like it Roger," Major Nelson moaned in ecstasy. "Clean up my nuts for me Healey, clean 'em up real nice and spit-shined…"

Hearing the words "Spit-shined", the captain did just that. He hacked up as much saliva as he could into his mouth, spit and dribbled onto the major's big sweaty balls as they dangled in front of him like ornaments on a Christmas tree and then alternately sucked the gonads in and out of his mouth, licking and polishing them as he had been ordered to.

"AWWW yeah, fuck man, your underlings sure as fuck taught you the way to treat your CO's balls Healey," Major Nelson groaned loudly and pressed his testicles harder yet against his charge's trembling lips and flicking tongue. "FEELS better than awesome...YEAH!!!"

After the major decided that his balls were good and cleanly licked he let go of Captain Healey's hair and stepped over to his desk. Captain Healey watched in tortured misery, all his hindquarters smarting beyond any pain he had ever felt before, as the major turned around and with his cock and balls still on display held up the thin wooden-handled hairbrush...

"Now Healey, I know just the CP you require at this point," the major chuckled as he approached the table that his underling still lay tied to at the wrists and ankles.

"OH GOD," the captain cried, sounding totally pitiful, and reached behind him to rub his poor ass cheeks and inner thighs... giving himself some needed relief...even if for a short moment...

A short while later Captain Healey found himself no longer splayed across the tabletop and tied to the legs of the table at the wrists and ankles. Rather, the beaten and befuddled army captain found himself now totally propped up atop the table and snugly and tightly hogtied, his wrists bound so close to his black socked calves that his chest area and his outer thighs were hoisted a tad up off the table. Captain Healey's muscular well-toned legs stuck straight up behind him...and the bottoms of his tied up socked feet seemed to be smiling up at the ceiling and he wiggled his toes miserably in those gold toed socks of his...

As the captain writhed and wriggled in the unforgiving unrelenting bondage he mumbled and murmured incoherently, not able to speak one word of intelligence…because as a final degradation before the next round of CP would begin, the captain's CO had stuffed his mouth with his cum soaked necktie and tied a length of rope over it, jamming the tie in the captain's mouth…effectively silencing him. Every time the captain chewed involuntarily on his necktie turned gag and swallowed he was treated to mouth and throat-full of the taste of his own spunk. As he writhed in the hogtie and every time he swallowed and tasted his spunk his cock and balls tingled underneath him.

"Okay Healey, now I'm sure you're wondering what all I was thinking when I decided to bind you up tighter than a drum like that," Major Nelson said, standing next to the table and holding his thin-handled hairbrush in hand and his other hand wrapped tightly around Captain Healey's trussed up left calf, caressing the material of his sock as he held his underling tight. "Not that I owe you an explanation mind you, but seeing as we go way back as buddies before we were CO and underling I feel it's only right that you should know why I do the things I do. And also, perhaps someday you may have to reprimand someone under your command in this fashion…so you can also look at this as a learning experience, bud."

"MMMFFFF…" was all the hogtied captain could say.

"I see you're in agreement with my having gagged you as well Healey," Major Nelson chuckled, sounding totally sadistic and squeezing the captain's calf tighter yet. "I do hope you're enjoying the taste of your own cum on that tie in your mouth bud."

Captain Healey simply rolled his eyes in his head, a feeling of total disbelief and shame consuming him. He chewed his necktie/

gag, swallowed, tasted his spunk and his cock and balls tingled and churned under him yet again.

"As the final part of your CP, I'm going to redden the bottoms of your feet under your dress socks Healey." the major said, rubbing the wooden handle of the hairbrush he was holding now against the bottoms of the captain's upturned tied up socked feet.

"RRRHHHMMMFFF…RHOOOO!!!   REEESSSEEE!!!" Captain Healey wailed behind the necktie/ gag in his mouth, trying to actually say, "NO, PLEASE!!!"

"And the reason for beating on your feet with this hairbrush is easily explained buddy," Major Nelson said as tears formed in the captain's eyes. "When you sit down you'll be reminded of this by the fact that I seared your ass red. When you put your uniform pants on you'll be reminded of this because I also seared your inner thighs red, along with your upper calves. Now, when you stand up and walk out of here very soon at this point you'll be reminded of this and your shortcomings with every step you take. And all of that searing I administered to you will remind you of what you will never do again…"

As the major spoke he raised the thin handled hairbrush high and above the captain's upturned socked feet.

"And what you will never do again, namely, is to make the men under your command suck your cock, or any other depraved ideas you might come up with to make them do," the major concluded and then brought the wooden handle of the hairbrush down HARD on the bottoms of Captain Healey's socked feet.

The hairbrush, like the cane earlier, made a swishing sound as it coursed through the air and then made hard and horrible contact with Captain Healey's feet.

SWISH CRACKKK SWISSSH CRACCCKKK SWISSSHHH CRACCCKKK SWWWIISSSH CRACCKKK SWWWISSSHHH CRACCCKKK

"HHHRRRRRMMMFFFFFF!!!" Captain Healey squealed, sputtering into his necktie/ gag, beads of spittle flying from the corners of his stopped up mouth. "MMMMEEEFFFFFF!!!"

The major held tight to one of Captain Healey's calves and over and over and over again brought his hairbrush down harder and harder with each blow on the bottoms of his charge's feet.

SWWWISSSHHH CRACK SWWWIIISSSHHH CRACKKK SWISSSH CRACCCK

SWIIISSSHHH CRACCCK SWIIISSHHH CRACCCK SWIIISSSH CRAAAACCCK

"RRRRRRRHHH!!!" Captain Healey wailed, sounding pitiful as tears streamed from his eyes and down his face like a waterfall.

"Army...captains...never...EVER...allow...their... underlings...to...suck...their...cocks..." Major Nelson panted as he cracked, cracked, swatted, swiped and beat his underling's feet relentlessly.

"RRRRRRMMMFFFFF...REBBBER ANAN!!!" Captain Healey roared behind his necktie/ gag, trying to say "Never Again!" to his major, to his commanding officer.

The captain's feet felt as if they had swelled up to twice their size in his socks as he lay there sweating, gasping for breath, screaming into his gag and crying like a kid as the major administered the final swatting blows to his upturned feet.

SWWWIIISSSH CRRRRAACCK SWWIISSSHHH CRACCCKKK SWIIISSSHHH CRACCCK

SWIIISSSHHH CRACCCK SWIIISSHHH CRACKKK SWIIISSSH CRAAAAAACK

"RRRRRRRMMMMM!!!" Captain Healey cried, and then panted and heaved as the major finally stopped beating his feet, dropping the hairbrush to the floor.

"Okay Healey, you've been disciplined," Major Nelson said breathlessly as he began undoing the ropes around Captain Healey's socked calves, sweating himself as he did so. "And I do hope you've learned a lesson from all this buddy."

As the major did his work untying him the captain nodded "YES" vigorously, numerous times...

Finally when he was untied the captain undid the rope around the necktie/ gag in his mouth and spit it out on the table in front of him as he lay there feeling miserable and exhausted.

"OH GOD, OH GOD SIR, that brush really stung," Captain Healey exclaimed, catching a glimpse of the major's steely erection as it stuck out hard and anew from the fly opening of his uniform pants.

"OF course it stung Healey, it was meant to sting," the major replied, talking as if the captain was the stupidest man on earth. "If it didn't sting I wouldn't have gotten my message across to you... and across your ass and thighs and calves and feet...HAR, HAR for you Healey!"

"God but I hurt everywhere," the captain whimpered, and as he lay on his stomach on the major's conference room table he reached behind him and rubbed his wounded ass cheeks and inner thighs. He propped his feet up on his socked toes as the stinging coming from the bottoms of them felt beyond immense. Actually, it felt to the well-disciplined captain that his feet were swelling up beyond reason in his black dress socks...

Then, without another word, the major reached down, grabbed Captain Healey by his inner thighs, clenched his hands tight around them, and dragged his buddy across the table, toward him, his asshole dragged directly toward the major's pulsing erection.

"UHHH, OH GOD…" Captain Healey bellowed and let go of his ass cheeks as he was dragged easily across the conference table, being that his body was slick with sweat.

Once his ass was dangling over the edge of the table Captain Healey felt his commanding officer's iron-like rod penetrate him, hard and deep…

"AAARRRHHH, JEEZ," Captain Healey panted as his commanding officer speared him hard and thick through his rear door.

"Oh fuck yeah Healey, I just love plowing an underling soldier's shit chute after he's been thoroughly disciplined," the major panted, gripping Captain Healey's thighs as his rod slid in and out of his underling's opening.

"OOOOOOHHHRRRR but it hurts SIR, it really hurts!!" the captain bellowed in anguish, as the major's thick steely erection slid against the sides of his spanked reddened asshole.

Memories of the rubber hose being used to spank his inner hole wreaked havoc in the captain's mind as his major was merciless as he plowed him harder and deeper with each thrust.

"OOOOOWWWOOOO…" Captain Healey howled, literally.

"You need to learn Healey, never allow your underlings to do this to you," the major intoned and meanly squeezed the captain's red welted ass cheeks as he fucked him harder and harder. "Oh yeah Healey, going to feed you more of my spunk, through your asshole this time bud, HARRRRR!!!"

"I've learned SIR, believe me, you've taught me well and I've learned..." the captain wailed, as tears once more flowed from his eyes and down the cheeks of his boyishly handsome face.

"OH YEAH, getting there now Healey, gonna feed you a good meal back here," Major Nelson panted, gave his underlings red ass cheeks a few open handed swats and then he was spurting rope after thick rope of his soldier jazz into his underling. "OH FUCK, yeah, yeah Healey, your fucking hole is tighter than my wife's pussy bud! HARRRRRRR!!!"

As Major Nelson shot his load and shot his load inside his charge Captain Healey found himself gyrating himself against his own erection under him as he lay on the table being fucked like some cheap whore on a Saturday night.

The major hoisted the captain's legs up by his socked calves and buried his spurting cock deeper yet inside his buddy.

"OOOOOOOO FUCK Healey," the major swooned and wiggled and waggled his muscular body real sexily as he thrust hard and deep inside Captain Healey.

As the captain took his major's cock the pain in his ass walls was unspeakable, yet even as he was fucked and even as he felt the major's load filling his hole the captain himself felt himself cumming as well...

The sounds of two men, two robust soldiers cumming and shooting their loads at the same time was nearly deafening in the major's office conference room...

When the major could shoot no more of his good stuff he let his shriveling cock slip slowly from his underling's opening.

"Well Healey, I do hope that all of this tonight taught you a much-needed lesson," Major Nelson said as he packed his spent cock and balls back into his uniform pants and zipped up.

"You can definitely say that Sir," Captain Healey said, still crying from the pain inside his shit chute. "With your permission Sir, may I get down off the table?"

"I don't see why not bud," Major Nelson said. "It should be fun to watch you tryin' to walk on those hairbrush spanked tootsies of yours, HARRRRRRR!!!"

"Thank you Sir," the captain whimpered and pressed his palms down against the tabletop.

As he raised himself up and off the table the major saw the mess of cum that his underling had spurt while having had the bottoms of his feet spanked...

"FUCK HEALEY, you really are one sleazy bastard aren't you?" Major Nelson asked with a smirk.

"I-I suppose you could say that Sir," Captain Healey replied, looking shamefacedly at his superior officer.

"Clean up my table you sleazy fuck," the major ordered. "And just be lucky that I don't decide to wallop that ass of yours all over again..."

"Y-YES SIR MAJOR NELSON, SIR!" Captain Healey sputtered, climbed down off the table and landed on his much wounded feet. "OWWW!!! DAMN, my poor feet!!!"

Then, a few seconds later, standing balanced on his toes and leaning over the table the captain dutifully slurped up his mess from his CO's table...

"Can't rightly believe just how fucking sleazy you really are Healey," Major Nelson chuckled. "When I ordered you to clean up my table just now I meant with rags and some other such items, but you took it upon yourself to lap it up like a dog, DAMN!"

When the captain left the major's office a short while later he scurried down the hall on his toes, in just his tall socks, his hands placed strategically over his soft cock and dangling balls. Major Nelson had kept Captain Healey's cum soaked necktie, as evidence, or so he claimed. The captain thought how more than likely the major wanted some sort of kinky souvenir of his conquest over him.

"OOOOOOWWWOOOOO…" the captain howled, praying that no one was working overtime at the base that night, still feeling disbelief over all that had transpired and happened to him. "A nice soak in a tub of cool water should relieve all this burning…"

When he reached his office he was glad to find the door unlocked. When his superior officer had taken him out of the office earlier he had been blindfolded and wasn't sure the major had left the door unlocked for him. Seeing as he was socks ass naked and could not have possibly carried keys anywhere the captain was totally relieved as he entered his office…walking on his gold toed toes only, seeing as the pain in the bottoms of his feet was beyond immense…and when he entered his office he felt a strange mixture of feelings at the sight of the two privates who had been servicing him when the major had abruptly walked in on them.

"OH JEEZ, you two, still here?" Captain Healey asked at the sight of the two privates sitting on the couch in his office, both of them with looks of guilt etched on their young handsome faces. "After the major caught us and scurried me off to his private office I thought that you two would have high-tailed it out of here."

As the captain spoke he stood awkwardly on his gold toed toes and slammed the door to his office shut. He then propped himself up against the wall next to the door.

"You two shouldn't be here," Captain Healey said, but there was no denying the tingling he was feeling in his cock as he looked at the two handsome fresh-faced young men.

The captain also noted that his cum smeared uniform jacket, along with the rest of his military attire were neatly hung on the man's clothes horse that he kept in his office.

"Uh, I see you hung up my uniform eh?" the captain asked as he wiggled on his toes, his cock stiffening between his legs and watched as his two underlings stood up from the couch.

The two young men were neatly clad in their uniforms, but as they stood up the captain saw that their cocks and balls were hanging out of the fly openings of their uniform trousers, pre cum oozing as well. The captain licked his lips and looked at the two men as they approached him.

"Fuckers, the major really worked me over for what he caught us at," the captain said breathlessly, trying to maintain his authority, but failing miserably. "Why'd you two have to make me cum by squeezing my goddamned foot like that? You know how that always gets me and...and..."

But then, the captain's words were cut short as the two privates moved his hands away from his semi-erect cock and Captain Healey then found himself leaning against the wall, still on his toes and panting in ecstasy as the two privates each slurped one of his nipples into their mouths.

"OOOOO, no, no you guys, we can't be doing this... OOOOO..." Captain Healey swooned. "I mean, we, we can't be doing this...we'll, I'll, I'll get my ass beat again...and...OH JEEEEZZZ..."

"Glad the major didn't whip his nipples," the first private said comically to his buddy and quickly slurped the captain's nipple back into his greedy mouth.

As his nipples were being serviced Captain Healey gyrated himself sexily on his socked toes and when the two privates reached around him and each grabbed one of his red ass cheeks in hand and squeezed them he nearly jumped out of his socks...

"OOOOHHH, easy with my butt cheeks you guys, the major really reddened them," the captain panted as he then caressed the tops of the two men's peach-fuzzed heads.

The sounds of slurping and sucking at nipples filled the room as the captain was serviced once again by the two privates...

A few moments later Captain Healey was lying on his back on his desk with his legs and thighs in the air, exposing his reddened ass cheeks for the two privates.

"OHHH, that feels so soothing, better than the cool tube of water I was going to lie in," the captain swooned as the two privates licked and lapped his red welted ass cheeks.

"Man, Major Nelson sure wasn't playing around Captain Healey," the second private said. "Even your thighs are all red...not to mention your asshole..."

That said the two privates took turns spreading Captain Healey's ass cheeks apart, exposed his swollen ass walls and plunged their tongues inside him, licking him almost ferociously, eating his ass like it was a buffet of sorts.

The captain squirmed atop his desk and slowly stroked his cock...which was at full mast by then...

"We, we shouldn't be doing this, OH GOD, we really shouldn't, but it feels so good, so soothing," the captain whimpered breathlessly as the two men took turns licking his ass walls. "After this you need to lick my feet too, the major really walloped them, with a thin handled hairbrush and..."

But suddenly the captain heard his office door slam shut loudly and then the booming voice of Major Nelson filled Captain Healey's office...

"HEALEY, GODDAMNIT MAN!!!" the major roared and the two privates instantly stopped what they were doing and knelt at the captain's now dangling calves and socked feet.

"Major Nelson, Sir, this time it wasn't my fault, they uh, they accosted me and…" the captain began but one of the privates quickly squeezed one of the captain's dangling feet…and the captain shot a load. "OOOOOOOO, I-I've been tricked again…UHHH…"

"And you'll be punished again as well Healey, and this time it will be your two sexy boy toys here that will be doing the honors," Major Nelson thundered.

The two privates grinned meanly across at each other…

As the captain squirmed on the table, shooting his load all over his chest and stomach areas he felt the tears welling up in his eyes as the major said, "Meet me with the captain in the officer's gym in ten minutes…"

Ten minutes later, in the officer's gym, Captain Healey found himself hoisted up off the floor and tied in a most heinous position to the man-sized punching bag that hung from the ceiling of the gym. The captain's upper body was roped tighter than tight to the punching bag and his muscular arms were pulled meanly around the punching bag and tied off at the wrists behind. His legs were curled up at the sides of the punching bag and tied off to the bag at the calves and upper thighs with mounds upon mounds of rope…

As the two privates did the chore of securing their captain to the punching bag, Major Nelson stood nearby supervising their work, holding the captain's tall black socks in one hand as he watched his buddy being tied most painfully and snugly.

"What have you got to say for yourself now Roger?" the major asked.

"Major Nelson Sir, I am so sorry, if you would only permit me to explain," Captain Healey began and in response the major held up the captain's socks, which he himself had had the pleasure of peeling off his buddies feet just moments before…revealing the very reddened bottoms of those feet at that.

"Nothing to explain Roger, you obviously need more CP," the major said.

"OH GOD PLEASE SIR!!!" Captain Healey begged.

"SILENCE HEALEY!" the major blurted angrily. "If it's the last thing I do I will teach you how to be a proper and respectful soldier…"

Moments later Captain Healey was tied to the punching bag…and gagged…with one of his tall socks crammed in his mouth and its mate tied over it, jamming it in place. Captain Healey rolled his eyes in his head as he involuntarily chewed on his sweat and rancid tasting sock…and every time he swallowed he was treated to a mouth and throat-full of his own foot stink.

"Okay boys, here is what you two are going to do," Major Nelson then said as he stepped over to supply cabinet.

He opened the long supply cabinet and Captain Healey cringed in the bondage he was securely tied in and his eyes opened wide in terror when he saw what his CO took from the supply cabinet…

As Major Nelson handed a riding crop each to the two privates Captain Healey looked woefully down at his jutted up nipples. It was just too unthinkable…and too ironic at that…seeing as one of the privates had so comically said earlier that it had been a good thing that the major had not beat his nipples…and now the two privates would…

"MMMFFFFFFF..." Captain Healey wailed as the two privates approached him with the thin riding crops in hand.

A few moments later the sounds of the riding crops swishing through the air and the tips of them connecting with the captain's nipple tips filled the air of the military gym.

"RRRRRRRMMMFFFFEEEFFFFF!!!" the captain squealed crazily as his poor nips were brutally tortured.

The major stood by watching, supervising as the two privates did their work...and the major had a new steely boner tenting his uniform trousers at that...

THE DEPUTY BY ALAN SKRAM

Written by Alan Skram

This is my first story...

———————————

This is actually a quick story about a guy that visits a small, rural town for his wife's class reunion, not me of course, but someone I know. (Isn't that what everyone says? Not me, someone I know?) His wife went to school in a small Oklahoma town, but they met when she moved to the big city. He is staying in the only hotel, in a town that has only one main street. He goes back to the hotel room and leaves his wife with her girlfriends to catch up. They are going to be there all weekend and even though he's bored he is a devoted husband and supports his wife in every way. He sits in the chair on the second floor hotel room and turns on the TV. There's nothing on that captures his interests so he continues to flip the channels. By then it's about 11PM and he notices someone walking the main street and checking all of the businesses doors. From what the guy can see by streetlamp only he is suddenly impressed. It looks to be a young handsome deputy; he'd guess his age to be around 25, with dark hair and a really nice build. He is wearing a sheriff's uniform button down shirt but instead of slacks he is wearing tight Wrangler's jeans and cowboy boots. The guy can't believe it. Here he is in Hicksville where, he assumes, nightly, the sheriff's young handsome deputy still walks the beat…in a goddamned one-horse town at that. The guy finds that he cannot take his eyes off this handsome V-shape in uniform and his heart beats with anticipation as the hot, handsome deputy walks between streetlamps. Each time his eyes try to take in more details as he moves from store to store to store front, in and out of the shadows.

The next day the guy tells his wife that he is going to walk around town, just to have something to do. This is her reunion after all he explains to her and he doesn't know any of the other out-of-town husbands. There were a couple of nice looking husbands that were visiting that weekend as well but they mostly stayed in the bar, drank, and watched sports television. The purpose of his walk was just to relieve the excitement he had felt the previous night watching the hot, masculine and handsome deputy make rounds. The previous night was Thursday and they had gotten into town and his wife's friends had pre-planned to meet at the hotel bar, which apparently seemed to be the only place they could meet, unless you considered the feed store at the end of the block. He walked slowly, following in the footsteps of the deputy he had seen the night before.

The next night was Friday. He made an excuse to go to the hotel room and his wife didn't seem to mind. He had been there for the picnic, the social hours, and visiting the old high school. So why not? He had been told on many occasions that he was very attractive, well educated, worked out regularly, and that his wife was very lucky to have him. He took some aspirin, just because he had told her he'd had a headache and took his seat next to the window. He then waited to see if the events unfolded as they had the previous night. He turned on the TV but couldn't afford to watch it, just in case someone made rounds early. 10:50, 10:57, 11:00, 11:02, 11:09 and still no sign of any movement. Maybe they do rounds randomly he thought to himself, and just then, out of the corner of his eye something moved on the sidewalk across the street. YES, it was the same deputy as before. All he could make out was the V-shaped body, the dark hair under the baseball cap and the outline of the boots he wore. He watched him stop at exactly the same door, in the same manner as the night before and probably every night since he started working. The deputy stopped and jiggled the door on the bakery; satisfied that it was secure he turned and looked across the street to the hotel entrance. As if moved by the will of him looking at the deputy the officer stepped towards the street and under direct light from the streetlamp removed his baseball cap and ran his hand across his brow, as if removing sweat from his forehead. There he was, as built as and even more handsome than he originally thought. Dark hair, the taut, tan, uniform shirt that clung to his body as if a second skin of clothing had been placed on his broad shoulders and small waist. The deputy smiled and waved at someone across the street, either entering or exiting the hotel. And he had a perfect smile to boot. The deputy, unaware of the show he was performing, or maybe he was, but from the interaction with other people he did not appear to be self-absorbed, as so many hot, well-built guys are, but he wasn't really interested in his personality, was he? The guy thought,

"I bet that boy gets all the pussy he wants in this little podunk town. He could have anyone he wanted in any town!" The deputy turned around and stepped away from the street light to resume his beat. As he turned the light fell on his back and shoulders but shadows appeared in the small of his back just below the belt. The light had landed on the roundest, firmest looking man ass the guy had ever seen. It was perfectly packaged in those tight Wranglers that fit him snugly in the waist, hips and thighs but then filled out a little to go over his boots. The jeans were just long enough so that the fabric scrunched a little where it rested on top of the boot. He continued to watch the deputy make the same, exact rounds as the night before. "I might need to make this young man's acquaintance," he thought to himself.

Saturday, their last night in town and the night of the big dance, two-step, ho-down, whatever they called it out in the sticks. The event started with dinner, dancing, and the obligatory "Who did…" awards. But thank goodness it started early. Apparently some of the classmates that still lived there had to get up early and plow, or something. He kept secretly looking at his watch waiting for the magic hour of 11PM. At 10:45 he told his wife that he was going to run upstairs and then step out for some fresh air. She had had one too many already and she wasn't known as someone who could hold their liquor. She kissed him on the cheek and he left her in the drunken hands of her high school girlfriends. He ran upstairs to their room and grabbed the small shaving kit he had prepared earlier. He tucked it under his suit coat and tried to look casual on the outside when his entire body was alive with anticipation of the events that were about to unfold. He made his way across the street and down two blocks from the hotel to the small, dark alley he had spotted on his previous walk-about-town. He arrived exactly at 11:00PM and set up his trap and awaited his prey. While sitting in the dark, hidden behind the dumpster he laughed to himself thinking, "What if tonight is his night off and some 90 year old man takes his place?" He told himself that he would be able to see the figure at the end of the alley in the light before they made their way into his clutches. He sort of felt like the villain in the old black and white movies that kidnaps the maiden and ties her to the railroad tracks, except he didn't have a handlebar moustache and his victim certainly was not a helpless maid. No, he had chosen a prime, young buck that could no doubt handle himself.

He heard footsteps approaching and he saw a figure at the entrance to the alley, and it was his hot, handsome deputy in all his masculine perfection. He pushed "Send" on his phone and a phone on the ground at the other end of the dumpster started to ring. It was his wife's cell phone that he had called from his cell phone. The deputy had just passed the alley entrance when the phone started ringing. He heard the deputy say, "What in the world?" as he turned and made his way to the ringing cell phone on the ground. The guy could see the flashlight beam scan the alley in search of the mystery ringing. The deputy then stooped to pick up the phone, stood up, and was just about to say, "I wonder who's phone is this?" when a gruff sounding voice told him, "Don't turn around, I've got a gun at your neck!" The deputy was about to say something when he was told, "Shut-up and do as you're told and you won't get hurt, do you understand me boy?!?" The deputy said, "Yes." The voice told him to get on the ground and to put his hands on top of his head.

"What do you want with me?" the deputy asked.

"Didn't I tell you to shut-up?" the guy asked in reply. "If I have to tell you again you'll be sorry, got it boy?"

"Yes," was the only response given.

The deputy then did as he had been instructed and laid on the ground, face-down with his hands on top of his head. The guy took the pen-light from his pocket and let the light slowly illuminate the prostate figure before him.

"I can't believe I'm really doing this," he thought to himself but the sight of this beautiful, bubble-butted, sexy, masculine man eroded every ounce of doubt that told him to leave.

From the bag he had hidden under his coat he pulled a length of rope which he had acquired down by the feed store. He knelt beside the deputy and put the gun to his cheek and said, "Are you a smart boy who is going to do as he is told or are you someone whose family will have to make funeral arrangements?"

"I'll do what you say, just don't hurt me man," was the response which he took as an "I'll do as told." "Now, slowly put both your hands behind you and don't make any sudden movements' boy!"

The deputy, with his face turned away from him slowly removed his hands from his head and placed them behind his back. The deputy's body jumped from surprise and shock and air hissed through his clenched teeth as he felt the rope bind both his hands together, but he didn't say a word. The guy then pulled out a plastic shopping bag that he had gotten out of the dumpster and used it to blindfold his newly acquired interest.

He put the gun; I mean the magic marker back into his coat pocket.

"Now boy roll over," was the command the bound and blindfolded deputy heard.

The deputy crossed his legs and using his bent knees rolled onto his back.

"Please, what do you want?" issued from his mouth, sounding whispered and shaky.

"You'll know soon enough, boy," the guy replied.

He took the pen-light, shone on his prone bound up blindfolded deputy and took in every perfect detail of the officer's body. When the light hesitated over the very large bulge that was so prominently and deliciously displayed in his Wranglers jeans it was all the guy could do not to lose control.

"Damn! That's a big dick you got there boy!" the guy laughed.

And with that the deputy pulled his legs together, I'm assuming at an attempt to keep the guy from gaining access to it. Witt that the guy jumped atop the deputy's body and shoved his hand over his mouth.

"Now listen boy, if you know what's good for you you'll give me what I want and I'll be on my way and you'll live another day," the guy seethed in the blindfolded deputy's face.

Through his hand-gag the guy could make out the words, "You fucking faggot, I'm going to kick your ass," as the deputy's body bucked and squirmed, trying to rid itself of this faggot parasite. This wasn't his first rodeo so the guy pushed his legs between the deputy's legs...and forced them open. The deputy tried to scream but the hand clamped further down on his mouth and he felt cold metal push against his throat.

"Shut-up or I'll slit your throat boy," the guy threatened. "The sooner you realize I'm going to get what I came for when I captured you the better off you'll be. Now, do you want them to find your body in this alley with your throat slit? I don't want to do that, but I will if you make me. Now, I'm going to take my hand away and if you try to scream it will be your last…and if you don't I'll know we have an understanding."

He removed the blade of his little pocket knife and not sure of which option the deputy had chosen, so he slowly removed his hand from the stud's mouth. The deputy didn't say anything so the guy chuckled, "Good choice boy, I'd really hate to mess something as hot as you up."

"Now, let's see what we have here," the guy said as his hands began to explore the bound and blindfolded deputy's rock-hard body.

His hands ran lustfully over the tight, tan uniform shirt, feeling the perfect pecs, down to the washboard stomach and then taking the deputy's bulge in hand. The deputy's body lurched forward and he hissed at his captor, but he did not try anything. He gave the deputy's dick a few squeezes and he said, "As nice and big as that feels that's not what I'm really after, but I bet you get your share of pussy don't you boy? A big handsome stud like you, the ladies must just be throwing themselves all over you and in uniform at that, DAMN! Ladies love that huh boy?" He softly laughed because tonight this deputy was his pussy. He started to undo the deputy's belt and the stud kicked up one knee in an attempt to thwart off his captor's advances.

"Tisk, tisk, boy, don't do that again or you'll be sorry and there are no more warnings at this point," the guy said laughingly.

The deputy's long muscular leg stretched out and he seemed to resign himself to his fate at hand. The guy then unbuckled the deputy's belt, then his jeans…and then pulled down the zipper. The deputy froze his muscular body stiff as a board as he lay there…and he never made a sound or movement unless directed by the guy who had so easily captured him. The guy yanked the snug Wranglers down off the muscular hips of the deputy whose body bucked with every attempt not to let the guy expose his goldmine. The guy then rolled the deputy onto his stomach and there was the much coveted prize, the most perfect man ass he'd ever seen; round and full, not the kind that spreads from the hips but extends outward, almost the shape of half-moons, no pun intended, well maybe. He gave the deputy's Wranglers a few more tugs to pull them further down, thus exposing more of those perfect gateways to paradise. From his bag he removed some KY and a condom. It did not take long to get that condom over his already hard cock. He was not huge, but almost nine inches, and thicker at the base than at the top, cut, and he definitely had had no complaints from anyone, none that he knew of anyway. Although he was sure that this hapless deputy would complain. He lowered himself onto the helpless deputy, his dick cradled in the tight, round firmness of the officer's ass, sliding his body up and down, distributing the lube closer to heaven's gate. The deputy whispered, "You better think about what you're doing faggot, before you go too far." No whimpering, no "please let me go," no "please don't hurt me," no begging for mercy, none of that from this hunky guy. That sounded like a threat to the guy who had so expertly captured the deputy and with that he tore the back of the deputy's briefs off him and shoved his hard dick into the officer's hot, tight man pussy. The deputy automatically clinched every muscle in his body, including the one the guy was raping. Through clenched teeth the guy heard the sounds of whispered agony. That pussy was so tight that the guy had to force himself into the deputy over and over while at the same time he was trying to spread his legs to allow more entry. He wanted the deputy to have all of him because he was definitely taking all of him. With each thrust he shoved more and more of his hard dick further into the deputy's ass and with each thrust the guy grunted and hissed as the force of his entry shoved his body forward. Not once did the deputy cry out for help. He was giving the old phrase, "Take it like a man" new meaning. The guy had just worked all of his cock into the deputy's hot, virgin ass when he heard the sound of a walkie-talkie say, "Austin, you there? Can you go by old Mrs. Gordon's place when you get finished? She can't find her dog." He froze for a moment and then the guy reached over and took the walkie-talkie from the deputy's belt. He held it to the officer's face.

"You can tell him you're busy taking it up the ass if you want to boy," the guy snickered meanly. "Or you can tell him you'll be right there. Which will it be?"

With that the rapist pressed the call button and held the walkie-talkie to the deputy's mouth and waited. The deputy said, "I'll be there in a little while."

"Okay," came back over the walkie-talkie.

"Good boy," the guy said to the deputy. "Are you sure you don't want me to let you use the walkie-talkie to call for him for help? I want to hear you tell the department that you were captured and are too busy being a faggot's pussy boy."

"Go to hell," was the deputy's reply as he lowered his face back into the ground.

The guy's dick had gotten soft since the walkie-talkie distraction but all it took was a slap and a grab on that hot ass to make the deputy's butt twitch and to get things going again. This time he drove further and further with each thrust, meanly pulling completely out and then re-inserting his cock again into the hapless deputy's ass. He wanted to give the hot, handsome stud deputy the best fuck of his life, or at least one of the best of his. Either because the deputy's ass was so tight or his ass had quickly learned how to take a cock, the officer's butt seemed to clinch upon every entry and relax at every exit, regardless, this was a hot fuck. At last the guy could not hold back any longer, and with a few, final, deep thrusts, he let his cum flow like the Niagara Falls, almost filling the condom on his dick inside the hottest ass in the Midwest. When he was sated he got up, pulled the condom from his semi-hard cock and placed it in a zip-lock baggie for later disposal. He then zipped up his trousers. Squatting down next to his conquest he rolled the deputy onto his back. His stomach area pushed forward from having his hands bound up behind his back and the guy ran his hands over the helpless deputy's body, still amazed how each ab was so sexily defined…and the flatness of his hard stomach. In one hot movement he leaned down further and slurped the deputy's cock into his mouth, engulfing the fat, man meat into his gullet and sucked it as though he was suffocating and air issued from it. The deputy's head and body jerked and in an exhausted gasp he simply said, "Please."

"Please what boy?" the guy asked the blindfolded bound deputy. "You want me to suck you more or quit? From the reaction of this beautiful cock you've got I think I know the answer…"

And with that the guy ran his mouth up and down the hard, cut cock of the deputy…until he exploded in a total wave of body spasms.

"Thanks for the fuck Deputy, and good day to you," the guy said as he quickly gathered everything he had brought with him, walked to the end of the alley, looked around and not seeing anyone, disappeared into the dark night.

Back in the hotel room as he was showering the guy looked at the trophy sitting on the edge of the tub, it was the deputy's badge.

"Now I have one more for my collection," the guy said to himself.

When he got out of the shower his wife was in bed, the alcohol making her sleep like the dead. He had very pleasant dreams himself that night, which included a dream of a deputy named Austin and the best fuck of the month. Well, next month he might need to meet Officer Ritchie, the cop that worked part-time at his bank…

He woke up the next morning, no thoughts of police breaking down the door, road barriers, or DNA testing. Guys like Deputy Austin were not the kind to tell anyone that a faggot had gotten the best of them, and he had laid there like a bitch and gotten fucked…

Now back to the city and Officer Ritchie…

ABOUT THE AUTHOR

Christopher Trevor was born in July 1963 and grew up in New York City. As soon as he was old enough to know how he began writing fiction and has been writing gay erotic/fetish stories for the past ten to twelve years at this point. He became an avid reader as well from the time he knew how and reads everything from fiction, to non-fiction to biographies of interesting and unusual  people, people who have made a difference or who have paved the way for others. Christopher attributes his writing artistic inspiration to artists such as Etienne, Tom of Finland, Tagame, The Hun, and most notably Joe T, who Christopher has had the pleasure of speaking with and even meeting over the last few years. Christopher states, "Joe T encouraged me to write about my fetish because I was embarrassed about it at the time. Joe T said that when we are embarrassed about something that makes it even more enticing somehow." Christopher totally agreed and never stopped writing in this genre. Erotic writers who inspired Christopher Trevor were: Tom Shaw (author of "That Day at the Quarry), C.S. White (author of Big Sur), Larry Townsend (author of countless erotic novels), and Mason Powell (author of the classic story "The Brig.")

Christopher discovered that not only did he enjoy writing erotic tales but that after his first bondage experience he had a genuine flair for it. Writing to erotic oriented magazines about his first bondage experience truly opened the floodgates for Christopher where this style of writing is concerned. Christopher thanks the handsome and muscular "Greg" for that experience way back in time. Christopher took "Creative Writing" courses every semester during his high school years and while other friends of his stopped writing what they loved to write about as time went on Christopher never let a day go by when he didn't write something... "I feel that if I don't write every day I will die," Christopher has said many times over.

Foot fetish stories and all things related; spanking fetish, erotic shaving, muscle bondage, tickle torture, and hardcore stories are just a few of the areas of gay eroticism that Christopher enjoys writing about and inspiring in others as well. As one internet buddy said to Christopher where the black socks fetish is concerned, "Until I started talking with you I never gave a thought to my socks when I got dressed for work in the morning. Now when I pull my dress socks on every morning I get a chill up my spine."

Christopher is proud of the erotic effect he has on people...

Christopher Trevor is also the author of:

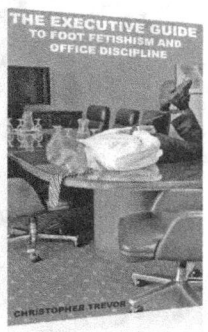

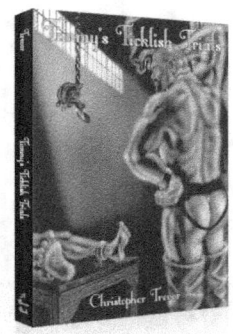

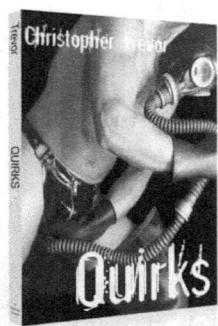

HUMILIATION
Christopher Trevor

a tribute to
Leather

Edited and Compiled by
Christopher Trevor

DISCIPLINE
COMPILED BY
Christopher Trevor

CLEEVE AND OTIS
STRIKE AGAIN
CHRISTOPHER TREVOR

REVENGE
Christopher Trevor

MEN AT WORK
CHRISTOPHER TREVOR

Quirks II
Christopher Trevor

OBSESSIONS
Edited by Christopher Trevor

MEN AT WORK II
CHRISTOPHER TREVOR

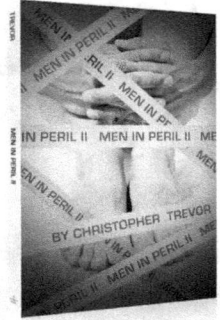

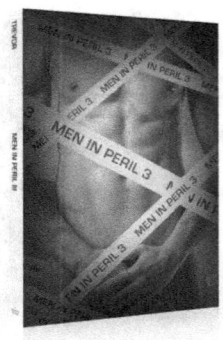